Diary of a Murderer

ALSO BY YOUNG-HA KIM

I Have the Right to Destroy Myself

Your Republic Is Calling You

Black Flower

I Hear Your Voice

Diary of a Murderer

AND OTHER STORIES

Young-ha Kim

Translated from the Korean
by Krys Lee

MARINER
BOOKS

An Imprint of HarperCollins*Publishers*

Boston   New York

First Mariner Books edition 2019

Copyright © 2013 by Young-ha Kim
English translation copyright © 2019 by Krys Lee

Mariner Books
An Imprint of HarperCollins Publishers, registered
in the United States of America and/or other jurisdictions.

www.marinerbooks.com

Library of Congress Cataloging-in-Publication Data
Names: Kim, Young-ha, 1968– author. | Lee, Krys, translator.
Title: Diary of a murderer : and other stories / Young-ha Kim ;
translated from the Korean by Krys Lee.
Description: Boston : Mariner Books, 2019.
Identifiers: LCCN 2018042555 (print) | LCCN 2018046728 (ebook) |
ISBN 9781328545565 (ebook) | ISBN 9781328545428 (paperback)
Subjects: LCSH: Kim, Young-ha, 1968—Translations into English. |
BISAC: FICTION / Literary. | FICTION / Short Stories (single author).
Classification: LCC PL992.415.Y5863 (ebook) |
LCC PL992.415.Y5863 A2 2019 (print) | DDC 895.73/5—dc23
LC record available at https://lccn.loc.gov/2018042555

Book design by Kelly Dubeau Smydra

Printed in the United States of America

23 24 25 26 27 LBC 9 8 7 6 5

This book is published with the support of the
Literature Translation Institute of Korea (LTI Korea).

CONTENTS

Diary of a Murderer

DIARY OF A MURDERER

It's been twenty-five years since I last murdered someone, or has it been twenty-six? Anyway, it's about that long ago. What drove me back then wasn't, as people usually assume, the urge to kill or some sexual perversion. It was disappointment. It was hope for a more perfect pleasure. Each time I buried a victim, I repeated to myself: I can do better next time.

The very reason I stopped killing was because that hope vanished.

•

I kept a journal. An objective report. Maybe I needed something like that at the time. What I'd done wrong, how that made me feel. I had to write it down so I wouldn't repeat the same gut-wrenching mistakes. Just like students keep a notebook with all their test mistakes, I also kept meticulous records of every step of my murders and what I felt about them.

It was a stupid thing to do.

Coming up with sentences was grueling. I wasn't trying to be literary and it was just a daily log, so why was it so difficult? Not being able to fully express the ecstasy and pity I'd felt made me feel lousy. Most of the fiction I'd read was from Korean-language textbooks. They didn't have any of the sentences I needed. So I started reading poetry.

That was a mistake.

The poetry teacher at the community center was a male poet around my age. On the first day of class he made me laugh when he said solemnly, "Like a skillful killer, a poet is someone who seizes language and ultimately kills it."

This was after I'd already "seized and ultimately killed" dozens of prey and buried them. But I didn't think what I did was poetry. Murder's less like poetry and more like prose. Anyone who tries it knows that much. Murdering someone is even more troublesome and filthy than you think.

Anyway, thanks to the teacher I got interested in poetry. I was born the type who can't feel sadness, but I respond to humor.

·

I'm reading the Diamond Sutra: "Abiding nowhere, give rise to the mind."

·

I took the poetry classes for a long stretch. I'd decided that if the class was lame I would kill the instructor, but thankfully, it was interesting. The instructor made me laugh several times, and he even praised my poems twice. So I let him live. He probably still doesn't know that he's living on borrowed time. I recently read his latest poetry collection, which was disappointing. Should I have put him in his grave back then?

To think that he keeps writing poems with such limited talent when even a gifted murderer like me has given up killing. How brazen of him.

•

I keep stumbling these days. I fall off my bicycle or trip on a stone. I've forgotten a lot of things. I burned the bottoms of three teapots. Eunhui called and told me she made me an appointment at the doctor's. While I yelled and roared with anger, she stayed silent until she said, "Something is definitely not normal. Something definitely happened to your head. It's the first time I've ever seen you get angry, Dad."

Had I really never gotten angry before? I was still feeling dazed when Eunhui hung up. I grabbed the cell phone to finish our conversation, but suddenly I couldn't remember how to make a phone call. Did I first have to press the Call button? Or did I dial the number first? And what was Eunhui's phone number? I remember there being a simpler way to do this.

I was frustrated. And annoyed. I threw the cell phone across the room.

•

I didn't know what poetry was, so I wrote honestly about the process of murder. My first poem, was it called "Knife and Bones"? The instructor remarked that my use of language was fresh. He said that its raw quality and the perceptive way I imagined death depicted the futility of life. He repeatedly praised my use of metaphors.

I asked, "What's a metaphor?"

The instructor grinned—I didn't like that smile—and explained "metaphor" to me. So a metaphor was a figure of speech.

Ah-ha.

Listen, sorry to let you down, but that wasn't a figure of speech.

I grabbed a copy of the Heart Sutra and began reading:

> So, in the emptiness, no form,
> No feeling, thought, or choice,
> Nor is there consciousness.
> No eyes, ears, nose, tongue, body, mind.
> No color, sound, smell, taste, touch,
> Or what the mind takes hold of,
> Nor even act of sensing.
> No ignorance or end of it,
> Nor all that comes of ignorance.
> No withering, no death,
> No end of them.
> Nor is there pain, or cause of pain,
> Or cease in pain, or noble path
> To lead from pain.
> Not even wisdom to attain!
> Attainment, too, is emptiness.

The instructor asked me, "So you really haven't studied poetry before?" When I responded, "Is it something one has to learn?"

he said, "No. Rather, if you have a bad teacher, it'll ruin your lines." I said, "That so? That's a relief." Then again, there are at least a few things in life you can't learn from others.

•

They took an MRI. I lay down on a medical table that resembled a white coffin and went into the light; it felt like a kind of near-death experience. I floated in the air and looked down at my body. Death is standing by my side. I understand. I am going to die soon.

A week later, I had some sort of cognitive abilities test. The doctor asked questions and I answered. The questions were easy, but answering them was hard. It felt like putting your hand in a fish tank and trying to catch a fish just out of reach. Who is the current president of Korea? What year is it right now? Please repeat the last three words you just heard. What is seventeen plus five? I was sure I knew the answers, but I couldn't remember them. How could I know but not know? How was this possible?

After the exam, I sat down with the doctor. He looked grim.

"The hippocampus has atrophied," he said, pointing at the MRI scan of my brain.

"It's unmistakably Alzheimer's. We can't be certain at this point how far it's progressed. We'll need to keep watch over time."

Next to me, Eunhui sat quietly, her mouth firmly shut.

The doctor said, "Your memories will gradually disappear. Your short-term memory and your recent memories will go first. It can be slowed but it can't be stopped. For now, take the prescribed medication regularly. And write everything down, and keep those notes on your person. In time you may not be able to find your own house."

•

I'm rereading a yellowed paperback copy of Montaigne's *Essays*. Reading it as an old man is surprisingly enjoyable: "We trouble life by the care of death, and death by the care of life."

•

On the way back from the hospital, we were stopped at a checkpoint. The policeman looked at Eunhui and me like he knew us, then sent us off. He was the youngest son of the village association leader.

He said, "We're running a checkpoint because there's been a murder. Working day and night with no end in sight is killing us. What do people think, that murderers wander around in broad daylight saying, 'Please catch me'?"

He then told us that three women had been murdered between our district and the neighboring one. The cops had deduced that it was the work of a serial killer. The women were all in their twenties and had been killed late at night on their way home. They had rope burns on their wrists and ankles. The third victim was found soon after my Alzheimer's verdict, so naturally I asked myself: Am I the murderer?

At home I flipped through my wall calendar and checked the suspected dates. I had foolproof alibis. I was relieved it wasn't me, but I didn't like knowing that someone was kidnapping and killing in my territory. I warned Eunhui that the murderer could be lurking among us. I told her what precautions to take and never to be out alone late at night. It would

6

be over for her as soon as she got into a man's car. And it was dangerous to walk with headphones on.

"Please don't worry so much," she said.

At the front door, she added, "It's not as if murders happen every day."

•

These days I write everything down. There are times when I find myself somewhere unfamiliar and stay confused until I get back home, thanks to the name-and-address tag hanging from my neck. Last week someone took me back to the local precinct.

The policeman greeted me with a smile. He said, "Sir, it's you again."

"You know me?"

"Of course. I probably know you better than you know yourself."

Really?

"Your daughter is on her way. We've already contacted her."

•

Eunhui graduated from an agricultural college and was hired by a local research center. She works on improving crop varieties. Sometimes she takes two different varieties and grafts them to create a new species. She practically lives at the research center, in her lab coat, and occasionally pulls all-nighters. Plants aren't interested in what time humans arrive at and leave work. Sometimes the pollination has to take place in the middle of the night. They grow this way, brazen and fierce.

People think that Eunhui is my granddaughter and act surprised when I say she's my daughter. That's because though I turned seventy this year, Eunhui is barely twenty-eight. The one most curious about this is none other than Eunhui. When Eunhui was sixteen, she learned about blood types at school. I'm type AB, but Eunhui is type O. For parents and their kids, that's an impossible combination.

"Dad," she asked, "how can I be your daughter?"

In general, I try to be as truthful as possible.

I said, "I adopted you."

That was around the time Eunhui and I started growing apart. She wasn't sure how to act around me anymore, and in the end we couldn't bridge the distance between us. After that day, we were no longer as close.

There's a condition called Capgras syndrome, which is caused by an abnormality in the part of the brain that controls intimacy. If you suffer from it, you're able to recognize the faces of people close to you, but you no longer feel you know them. For example, a husband will suddenly start to distrust his wife, saying, "You look just like my wife and act exactly like her—who are you really? Who put you up to this?" No matter the evidence, he'll think she's a stranger. She looks like a stranger to him. Before long, the patient will be forced to live with the feeling that he has been exiled to an unknown world. He will believe that these people with similar-looking faces are lying to him.

After that day, it was as if Eunhui began feeling that the small world surrounding her, the family that was made up of the two of us, was an unfamiliar one. Still, we continued to live together.

·

When the wind blows, the bamboo forest behind the house makes a clamor. I become tangled up in thoughts when that happens. On these windy days, even the birds go quiet.

I bought the tract of bamboo forest long ago. I never regretted it—I'd always wanted my very own forest. In the mornings I head out behind my house for a walk. You can't run in a bamboo forest. If you accidentally trip on something, you might even die. If you cut down a bamboo tree, its sharp, firm roots remain. That's why you have to constantly watch your feet when you're surrounded by bamboo trees. On my way back to the house I listen to the crackling of bamboo leaves underfoot and think about the people I've buried below. Those dead bodies become bamboo and shoot up toward the heavens.

•

When Eunhui was younger she once asked me, "Where do my birth parents live? Are they still alive?"

"They're dead," I said. "I brought you home from an orphanage."

Eunhui didn't want to believe me. She seemed to have searched the internet for information, even sought out the relevant government building, before locking herself in her room and crying for days. Then finally she accepted it.

She asked, "Did you know my parents?"

"We'd met before, but we weren't close."

"What kind of people were they? Were they good people?"

"They were wonderful. You were their main concern till the very end."

•

I pan-fry some tofu. I have tofu for breakfast, tofu for lunch, tofu for dinner. I drizzle the pan with oil and add the tofu. Once one side is cooked, I turn it over to the other side. I take out some kimchi, then have my meal. No matter how bad the Alzheimer's gets, I hope I can manage at least this much alone. A basic rice with tofu.

•

I was in a minor car accident. It happened at a three-way intersection, and the bastard's jeep was in front of me. These days, bad vision is part of my everyday life. It's probably the Alzheimer's. I didn't see the guy's car at a standstill, and before I knew it, I ran right into him. It was one of those jeeps custom-designed for hunting. As if searchlights on the roof weren't enough, he'd also mounted three sets of fog lights on the bumper. Such cars are remodeled so the trunk can be rinsed down with water. He'd also added about two extra batteries. When hunting season starts, guys like him flock to the mountains behind the village.

I got out of the car and walked over to the jeep. The driver didn't get out. He had his windows rolled up, so I knocked on the glass.

"Look here," I said. "Let's talk face-to-face."

He nodded and gestured as if to say, Just go on your way. That was odd. Didn't he at least want to check his rear bumper? When I didn't budge, he finally got out of the jeep. A short, stocky man in his early thirties. He quickly scanned the bumper and said it looked fine.

It wasn't fine. The bumper was dented.

He said, "Don't worry about it, sir. It was already dinged. It's really fine."

I said, "Just in case, let's exchange numbers. So there won't be trouble later."

I handed him my number, but he wouldn't take it.

"There's no need." His voice was low-toned, expressionless.

I said, "Do you live in the neighborhood?"

The guy didn't say anything. But for the first time he did look me straight in the eyes. He had the eyes of a snake. They were cold and cruel. I was positive: in that moment we recognized each other.

He neatly printed his name and number on a piece of paper. It was a kid's handwriting. His name was Pak Jutae. I returned to the rear of the jeep and checked the damage one more time. That's when I saw it: the blood dripping from the trunk. I also felt his gaze. That gaze studying me as I listened to the dripping blood.

If blood drips out of a jeep made for hunting, people tend to think it's carrying something like a roe deer. But I begin by assuming there's a dead person inside. It's safer to think this way.

•

Who was it again? A Spanish writer, or was it an Argentinian? I don't remember stuff like a writer's name anymore. Anyway, in some writer's novel, an elderly man walks by a river and ends up sitting on a bench, talking to a young person he's just met. Only later does he realize what's happened: the young person he met by the river is actually himself. If I had the chance to meet my younger self, would I recognize him?

•

Eunhui's mother was my last offering. On the way back from burying her, my car crashed into a tree and flipped

11

over. The police said that I was speeding and had lost control around a curve. I had to have brain surgery twice. Lying in the hospital bed, I felt so completely at peace. It wasn't like me. At first I thought it was because of the pills they gave me. Before, I became uncontrollably irritated if I even heard someone being loud. Noise had been almost unbearable. The sound of people ordering food, the sound of kids laughing, the sound of women gabbing—I hated it all. But now this sudden peace. I'd always thought my constantly seething mind was normal. It wasn't. Like a person who has gone deaf, I was forced to get used to this sudden stillness and peace. Whether it was from the impact of the crash or the surgeon cutting me up, something had happened to my brain.

•

Words are slowly escaping me. My head is turning into a sea cucumber. A hole is opening up. It's slimy and everything escapes through it. In the morning, I read the newspaper from beginning to end. After I finish reading, I feel as if I've forgotten more than I've learned. Still, I read. Each time I read a sentence, it feels like I'm forcibly assembling a machine that's missing a few crucial parts.

•

I'd had my eye on Eunhui's mom for a long time. She was an administrative assistant at my community center. She had lovely calves. Maybe it was the poems and the writing, but I felt I was getting soft. It was as if all this reflection and thinking were stifling my impulses. I didn't want to get soft or suppress the feelings boiling inside me. It was as if I were being shoved into a deep, dark cave. I just needed to know if I was who I knew myself to be back then. When I opened my eyes, I saw Eunhui's mother directly in front of me—chance is often the beginning of bad luck.

So I killed her.
But it wasn't easy.
It was disappointing.

A murder without any pleasure. Maybe whatever change was happening inside me had already started by then. The second brain surgery merely made it irreversible.

•

In the paper this morning, I read about another serial killing that shocked the local community. When were they saying the killing took place? Something was off, so I went through my notes and found I had jotted down information on the three earlier murders. Recently my memory's been more erratic than usual. Whatever I don't write down slips through my hands like sand. I jotted down the details of this fourth murder in my notebook.

A twenty-five-year-old female student was found dead on a country road. Her arms and legs were bruised with rope marks, and she was naked. Just like the others, she had been kidnapped, beaten, and left for dead by the roadside.

•

That jerk Pak Jutae hasn't called me. But I've seen him around a few times. Too frequent to call it a coincidence. And there must have been times when I saw but didn't recognize him.

He's prowling around my house like a wolf, watching my every move. If I approach him to talk, he quickly disappears.

•

Is he after Eunhui?

•

I've let more people live than I've killed. My father always used to say, "How many people in the world get to do whatever they want?" I agree.

•

It seems I didn't recognize Eunhui this morning. Right now I do recognize her. That's a relief. The doctor says that soon Eunhui will also disappear from my memory.

He said, "The only thing you'll remember is the way she looked as a child."

You can't protect someone you can't recognize, so I put Eunhui's photo in a pendant and hung it around my neck.

The doctor merely said, "No matter what you try, nothing will help. The recent memories go first."

•

Crying, Eunhui's mother begged me, "Please, at least spare my daughter."

I said, "Okay, then, don't worry about that."

I've faithfully upheld that promise until now. I hated people who made empty promises, so I tried hard not to become that kind of person. But the issue is now. I'm writing this down again so I won't forget: I can't abandon Eunhui to her death.

At the community center, the teacher taught a class using a poem by Midang. The poem was called "The Bride." In it, a groom is heading to the bathroom on his wedding night when his clothes get caught on the door latch. He flees, assuming his new bride is the lewd type and has grabbed at him. About forty years later he happens to pass by the same place and sees that his bride is still waiting there for him, so he nudges her, and she turns into a pile of ash.

The teacher and students alike went on and on about how beautiful the poem was.

I read it as a poem about a groom who kills his bride on their wedding night, then runs away. A young man and a young woman. And a dead body. How could you read it any other way?

•

My name is Kim Byeongsu. I turned seventy this year.

•

I'm not afraid of death. And I can't stop from forgetting. If I forget everything, I would no longer be the person I am now. If I can't remember who I am now, if there turned out to be an afterlife, how would that still be me? So it doesn't matter. These days only one thing occupies me: keeping Eunhui from getting killed before I completely lose my memory.

The karma, and the pratyaya, of this life.

•

My house is at the foot of a mountain, with its back turned from the main road, so passing hikers easily overlook it. Those on their way down are more likely to discover the house than

15

those going up. A large temple stands at the summit, and some people assume my house is a hermitage or temple lodging. There's the occasional dwelling a few hundred feet down the road. A couple with dementia lived in what the neighbors called the Apricot Tree House. At first it was just the husband who had dementia, but not long after, his wife received the same diagnosis. I don't know what others thought, but the couple did fine. Whenever I ran into them on the street, they would put their hands together respectfully and greet me. I used to wonder, Who did they think I was?

At first they thought they were living in the 1990s, but in their final years they traveled back to the '70s. Meaning, they returned to a time when one wrong word could get you imprisoned, a period of emergency measures and the so-called Makkoli Security Law. So when the two ran into strangers, they became guarded and cautious. To them, all the villagers were now strangers, and they found it bizarre that these unfamiliar people were constantly coming and going around them. Then it got to the point where the couple stopped recognizing each other. That was when their son showed up to put the old couple in a nursing home. One day I happened to pass by their house and witness the couple on their knees in front of their son, begging him to spare their lives, saying, "Please don't kill us! We're not Commies, we swear!" They seemed to have confused their son, who'd shown up wearing a suit, with a National Intelligence Service agent. The couple who could no longer recognize each other united in front of their son. The son alternated between being furious and tearful, until the neighbors stepped in and forced the old couple into the car that drove them away.

That could be my future.

•

Eunhui keeps asking me, "Why? Why are you like this? Why can't you remember? Why aren't you trying?" To Eunhui, I must be the very definition of strange. Sometimes she thinks I'm purposely making things difficult for her. She says I'm pretending not to know things, just to see how she will react. She says that I seem far too calm.

I know Eunhui cries alone when she shuts the door behind her. Yesterday I overheard her speaking on the phone with a friend. She said she was losing her mind.

She said, "He's not the same person. He's a different person today and different tomorrow. And he was different just now than from a moment ago, then a second later he's different again. Sometimes he's obviously got Alzheimer's, unable to remember what just happened, then other times he seems absolutely normal.

"He's not the father I used to know," she said. "I can't bear this. I can't stand it anymore."

•

My father was my genesis. My father, who beat my mother and my sister, Yeongsuk, whenever he drank: I smothered him to death with a pillow. My mother pressed down on his body and Yeongsuk on his legs. She was only thirteen. Rice husks burst from the sides of the pillow. Afterward, Yeongsuk refilled the pillow with the swept-up rice husks and my mother numbly stitched it up. I was sixteen when it happened. Sudden deaths were common after the Korean War. No one paid attention to a man who had died in his sleep at home. Not even a constable came

17

by. We set up a makeshift tent in the front yard and received mourners.

When I was fifteen I could carry a sack of rice on my back. In my hometown when a boy was strong enough to do that, not even his father could lay a hand on him. But my father still beat my mother and younger sister. He'd strip off their clothes and chase them out of the house in the freezing cold. Killing him was the best solution. The only regret I had was getting my mother and sister involved when I could have done it alone.

My father, who'd lived through the war, always suffered from nightmares. He also talked a lot in his sleep. Even as he died, he probably thought he was having another bad dream.

·

"Of all that is written, I love only what a person has written with his blood. Write with blood, and you will find that blood is spirit. It is no easy task to understand unfamiliar blood; I hate the reading idlers."

That's from Nietzsche's *Thus Spoke Zarathustra*.

·

I began killing when I was sixteen, and I continued until I was forty-five. I lived through the April Revolution and the May Massacre. President Park Chung-hee proclaimed the Yushin Reforms as he dreamed of making himself dictator for life. First Lady Yuk Young-soo was shot to death. President Jimmy Carter visited, told Park Chung-hee to abandon his dictatorial ways, then went jogging, wearing only underwear. Park Chung-hee was assassinated. Kim Dae-jung was kidnapped in Japan and narrowly escaped with his life. Kim Young-sam was expelled from the National Assembly. Martial law was declared in Gwangju, and the army laid siege to the city and beat and shot people to death.

Through it all I thought only about killing. I carried on a one-man war against the world. I killed, I fled, I lay low. I killed again, fled, and lay low. Back then there was no such thing as DNA testing or surveillance cameras. Even the term "serial killer" was little known. Dozens of suspicious-looking persons and the mentally ill were considered suspects, and were dragged off to the police station and tortured. A few even made false confessions. The precincts didn't cooperate with each other, so when a similar crime occurred in a different precinct, they didn't make the connection. Thousands of cops wielding batons climbed up the wrong mountains to investigate.

Those were good times.

⚫

I was forty-five at the time of my last murder. Looking back, it dawns on me that my father was also forty-five the year he suffocated under the pillow. What a strange coincidence. I'm writing this down, too.

⚫

Am I a devil, or a superhuman? Or both?

⚫

Seventy years of a life. When I look back, it seems that I'm standing in front of a gaping black cave. I feel little about my approaching death, but when I think about the past, my heart feels dark and vast. My heart was like a desert; nothing grew inside me. There was no moisture to be found anywhere. When I was younger, I tried to understand others, but it was too difficult a task for me. I always avoided eye contact so people assumed I was the shy and docile type.

I used to practice making faces in the mirror. A sad look, a happy look, a worried look, a dejected look. Eventually I developed a simple technique. I just imitated the person in front of me. If someone frowned, I frowned, and if someone laughed, I laughed.

In the old days, people thought the devil lived inside a mirror. The devil they saw in the mirror, he was probably me.

•

I had a sudden urge to see my sister. When I said this to Eunhui, she told me that my sister had passed away long ago.

"How did she die?"

"You know—she died after a long struggle with pernicious anemia."

It sounded oddly familiar, as if I'd heard this before.

•

I was a veterinarian. It's a good job for a murderer. You can use all kinds of powerful anesthetics. You can bring an elephant immediately to its knees. In the country, vets make a lot of house calls. While our city counterparts sit in clinics treating pet dogs and cats, in the country you travel around treating livestock, from cows and pigs to chickens. In the past, you even encountered the occasional horse. Outside of chickens, they were all mammals. There's not much of a difference between the human anatomy and theirs.

•

Once again, I found myself somewhere unfamiliar. A neighborhood I'd never been before. Some local kids surrounded me and put me in a storeroom, keeping me from going wherever it was I kept trying to go. They claimed I had been scared and caused a racket. A cop came, and after radioing in on his walkie-talkie, he took me away in his patrol car. I continue to forget and end up in strange neighborhoods, surrounded by locals, until the cops arrive.

The cycle repeats: the crowds, the encircling, the hauling off to the police station.

To an elderly serial killer, Alzheimer's is life's practical joke. No, it's a hidden-camera prank show. Surprised you, right? Sorry. It's only a joke.

•

I've decided to memorize a poem a day. It's not as easy as I'd thought.

•

I don't understand the new poems these days. They're too hard. But I do like the following line, so I'm writing it down:

"My pain cannot be read, for it does not have captions." From Kim Kyung-ju, "A City of Sadness."

From the same poem: "The times I lived were like bootleg liquor that no one had ever tasted. / I got easily drunk in the name of those times."

•

I was out shopping for groceries downtown when I spotted a familiar face prowling around Eunhui's research lab. I couldn't for the life of me tell who he was. It only came to me when I saw his jeep on my way home. It was that jerk. I took out my notepad and checked for his name. Pak Jutae. The guy had made his way to Eunhui.

•

I started exercising again. Generally, I focus on my upper body. The doctor had said that exercise would help slow down the Alzheimer's, but that wasn't why I began working out. It was for Eunhui. In a fight, what determines life or death is upper body strength. You seize, restrain, and choke. The weakest spot in mammals is the neck, where the trachea is. If oxygen doesn't reach the brain for a few minutes, you die or end up brain-damaged.

•

Someone I met at the community center once said that he liked my poems and that he'd like to publish them in a literary journal. This was over thirty years ago. I said, "Sure, go ahead," and not long after, I got a call. He said that the book was out and asked where he should send the copies. Then he read off his bank account information. When I asked if I had to pay for them, he said all the contributors do. When I replied I didn't like that, he whined, "The books are already printed, and if you do this to me now, it puts me in a bind." When he used the words "in a bind" so casually, I had a strong urge to correct him. But I had brought this situation on myself, with my bourgeois desires. It wasn't solely the guy's fault. Some days later, two hundred copies of a small regional publication with my poems in it arrived at my house. There was even a card tucked inside congratulating me on my debut. I saved one copy and used the rest for fuel. They burned well. My poem-heated floors kept me warm.

Anyway, after that I called myself a poet. The way you feel about writing poems that no one reads and committing murders that no one knows about is not that different.

•

While I was sitting on the wooden veranda waiting for Eunhui, I watched the sun set behind a distant mountain. I wondered if the sun's blood would soon stain the barren winter peak, but it quickly turned bleak. If I now enjoy things like this, it must be my time to go. I'll likely soon forget everything I've just seen.

•

They say that if you study human fossils from prehistoric times, you will discover that the majority were murdered. The most common clues are said to be holes bored into the skull or bones severed by sharp objects. Natural deaths were rare. Alzheimer's would have been near nonexistent: it would've been hard to survive to late middle age. I feel like a prehistoric human who somehow landed in this period he doesn't belong and where he has lived for far too long. My punishment is Alzheimer's.

•

Eunhui was once bullied at school. She didn't have a mother and her father was old, so the kids teased her. Without a mother, a girl doesn't know how to grow into a woman. The girls had a sixth sense for this and picked on her. One day Eunhui went to the school counselor for advice about a crush she had on a boy. By the following day, a rumor that Eunhui was obsessed with boys had spread across the school. The kids teased her, called her a slut. I read all this in Eunhui's diary. I had no idea what to do.

There are things that a serial killer can't put an end to: the bullying of a preteen girl.

I don't know how she got out of that situation. She's doing well now, so does that mean it's okay?

•

These days my father keeps showing up in my dreams. He sits at a low-lying wooden desk and begins reading something. My poems. With his mouth full of rice husks, he looks at me and laughs.

•

If my memory serves me right, I have lived with two women. The first woman bore me a son, but one day they both disappeared. Since she took our son when she fled, she might have sensed something in me. I probably could have found them if I really wanted to, but I left them alone. She wasn't the kind of woman worth reporting to the police. The second woman and I were actually married. We lived together for five years, until she said she couldn't stand me any longer and asked for a divorce. That she could speak so openly makes clear she had no idea what kind of person I was. I asked what was so wrong with me, and in what way, and she said, "You have no emotions. It's like living with a stone." The whole time, she was carrying on with another man.

A woman's facial expression is a difficult code to crack. It seemed to me that my wife always got worked up over nothing. If she cried, I got annoyed, and if she laughed, I got angry. When she went on about something, I would get so bored I could barely stand it. There were times I wanted to kill her, but I controlled myself. If a married woman ends up murdered, her husband is always the prime suspect. Two years after she left, I tracked down and killed my ex-wife and the bastard she'd had the affair with, dismembered them, and tossed them into a pigpen. Back then my memory wasn't like it is now. I never forgot what I wasn't supposed to forget.

•

Because of the number of serial murders in our area, a lot of crime experts are being featured on TV. A man who's supposed to be an expert profiler, or something like that, said: "A serial killer can't stop once he's begun. He ends up desiring an even stronger sensation, and tenaciously sets about hunting down his next victim. The addiction factor is so strong that even in jail, he thinks only about the next murder. If he starts believing that he won't be able to commit another one, he feels despair and tries to kill himself. That's how strong the drive is."

Experts only look like experts to me when they talk about things I know nothing about.

•

Eunhui keeps coming home late these days. I don't remember when I first heard about it, but Eunhui's research center is working on ways to grow tropical fruits and vegetables on Korean soil. They grow tropical fruits like papayas and mangoes in a greenhouse. There are many Filipino wives in every village who miss fruits they used to eat back home, so they sometimes stop by the center and gaze at the crops, and even pick the fruit.

Eunhui has never really gotten on well with people, and instead gives all her affection to the silent plants.

She once told me, "The plants give each other signals. When they feel threatened, they release a chemical odor to warn the others of danger."

"So they're emitting poison?"

"No matter how small a creature is, they all have a way of staying alive."

.

The dog next door keeps wandering onto our property. He shits and pisses in the yard. When he sees me, he barks. This is my house, you filthy mongrel.

The dog doesn't even run away when you throw a rock at him, but just hovers. When Eunhui returns from work, she says that the dog is ours. She's lying. Why would Eunhui lie to me?

.

I killed people for thirty years straight. I was very diligent back then. Now that the statute of limitations has passed, I could even go blab about what I'd done. If this were America, I could probably publish a memoir. People would attack me. Let them, if they want. It's not like I have many days left. I'm a tough one, when I think about it. After all those killings, I went cold turkey. I felt, well, like a boatman who'd just sold his boat, or a mercenary who'd just retired. I can't say for sure, but there must have been guys in the Korean or Vietnam War who killed more people than I did. Do you think they're all losing sleep over it? I don't think so. Guilt is fundamentally a weak emotion. Fear, anger, and jealousy are much stronger. Gripped by fear or anger, you won't be able to sleep. I laugh when I watch a movie or TV show with a character who loses sleep out of guilt. What are these writers trying to sell? They know nothing about life.

I quit killing and took up bowling. A bowling ball is round and firm and heavy. I like touching it. I bowled alone from morning to night until I could barely walk. The owner would signal my last game when he turned out all the lights except in my lane. Bowling is addictive. With each game, I feel I can somehow do a little better than the last time. I feel I can get the spare that I just missed, or raise my score. But I always end up with my usual score.

•

One of my walls is covered with notes. The multicolored notes stay where you stick them, and though I don't know where they came from, they're all over the house. Maybe Eunhui bought them to help my memory. These notes have a special name, but I can't remember it right now. The north wall is covered with them, and now the wall facing west is plastered with them, too, but they don't help much. They're mostly notes I don't understand, notes I don't remember sticking on the wall in the first place. Like the one saying, "Things you must tell Eunhui." What was it I meant to tell her? Each of the notes feels like a distant star in the universe. Nothing seems to connect them to each other. There's also one that the doctor wrote for me:

"Imagine it like a freight car hurtling along without knowing the rails are cut off ahead. What do you think will happen? Won't the train and the freight pile up where the tracks stop? And it will end in total chaos, won't it? Sir, this is exactly what's happening inside your head right now."

•

I remember an old lady I met in the poetry class. She told me that in the past—she emphasized this part—she'd had numerous love affairs: "I don't regret it. When you get old, you have all these memories. Whenever I'm bored I think about each of the men I slept with."

My life these days is just like that old lady's. I recall each person who died at my hands. There was also a movie about that: *Memories of Murder*.

•

I believe in zombies. There's no reason why something you can't see doesn't exist. I often watch zombie movies. I once kept an ax in my bedroom. When Eunhui asked why I kept an ax there, I said it was because of zombies. Axes work best on dead people.

•

The worst thing in the world is to be murdered. I can't let such a thing happen to me.

•

I hid the syringe in the sewing kit near my bed. A lethal dose of pentobarbital sodium. It's a drug used to put cows and pigs to sleep. I may use it on myself when I get to the point where I'm smearing my shit across the walls. I can't let it get that far.

•

I'm afraid. Frankly, I'm kind of afraid.

I'll read a sutra.

•

I feel so confused. When you start losing your memory, your mind starts to lose its way.

•

A poet named Francis Thompson wrote, "For we are born in other's pain, / And perish in our own." To my mother who gave me life, your son will soon die because his brain is riddled with holes. Or maybe I've got the human version of mad cow disease? Is the hospital hiding this from me?

•

For the first time in ages, Eunhui and I went downtown to a Chinese restaurant. We ordered lemon chicken and a mixed meat and seafood dish, but I had no idea what it tasted like. Am I losing my sense of taste as well? I asked Eunhui about work, but as always, she merely listened without saying it's sweet or bitter or anything definite. Eunhui spoke and acted as if nothing in the world had any effect on her. It's as if she were saying, *Yes, I do live there. And just like anywhere, there are people, things happen every day. But none of it has anything to do with me, and it doesn't really affect me.*

Eunhui and I have little to talk about. I don't know much about her life, and she doesn't know who I really am. But these days we do have one subject in common: my Alzheimer's. Eunhui is afraid of it. Because she's afraid, she keeps bringing it up. If my Alzheimer's gets worse but I live for a long time, Eunhui may have to quit work and take care of me.

What young woman wants to be stuck deep in the provinces, taking care of her demented old father? Since Alzheimer's is a degenerative disease, there's no hope for improvement. So my dying quickly would be good news for everyone. And, my Eunhui, if I die, there's more good news for you. You become the beneficiary of the life insurance policy I took out. Though you don't know about that yet.

I locked it in over ten years ago. The insurance saleswoman, who made a house visit after receiving my call, seemed surprised at the large amount of the policy. She looked in her mid-forties but seemed inexperienced. She was probably a housewife who'd raised her kids and gotten a late start in the insurance industry.

She asked, "Will your daughter be the sole beneficiary?"

I responded, "I don't have any other family. I had a sister, but she died young."

"It's good you're thinking about your daughter, but you should also prepare for your retirement."

"I'm already set for retirement."

"People live much longer on average than they used to. You should be prepared for the danger of living too long."

The danger of living too long. People these days really do excel at coming up with amusing phrases. I said nothing and just stared at the woman. I knew how to reduce the danger of living too long by a hundred percent. She must have seen something threatening in my eyes, for she shrank back a little.

"Well, do what you think best. But you should be preparing for retirement . . ."

She quickly spread out the documents for me to sign. I signed and signed. If I die, the insurance company has to pay out a huge sum to Eunhui. But what if she dies before I do? I can't stand the thought of Eunhui being dragged away and killed by someone. I know what that's like better than anyone.

•

I've never cursed anyone out. I don't drink or smoke either, so people always ask me if I'm Christian. There are fools who spend their whole lives putting everyone into categories. It makes things easy, but it's a little dangerous because they can't fathom people who don't fit into their flimsy boxes, like me.

•

In the morning, I opened my eyes. I didn't know where I was. I bolted up, pulled my pants on, and ran out. An unfamiliar dog barked furiously at me. I rushed around looking for my shoes, then saw Eunhui coming out from the kitchen. It was our house.

What a relief. I still remember Eunhui.

•

It happened about five years ago. I went to Japan on a hot springs tour with the old folks from the neighborhood. At Kansai International Airport, the immigration officer asked me, "What do you do?"

I don't know what I was thinking, but I said, "Killing people."

He glanced at me and asked, "Are you a doctor?" He had misheard "killing" for "healing." I nodded without saying anything, since a veterinarian is also a doctor. He said, "Welcome to Japan," and stamped my passport with a thump.

31

•

The only comfort is knowing I can die without pain. I'll be a drooling idiot before I die and won't even know who I am.

•

I've got a neighbor who blacks out after a night out drinking. Maybe death is a stiff drink that helps you forget the boring night out that is your life.

•

I happened to see a text message Eunhui sent her friend: "I'm going crazy. Each day is just too much to take."

Whether her friend was comforting her or being sarcastic, she texted back: "What a loyal daughter. Seriously, you're incredible."

"What's more terrifying is what might happen later. With Alzheimer's, they say your personality changes. I think it's already started."

"Send him to a nursing home. You said he's not even your real father, so why are you taking on the entire burden alone?"

The friend's texts continued. "Don't feel guilty. He won't remember anyway."

Eunhui's reply went like this: "They say Alzheimer's patients still have feelings."

I still have feelings. I still have feelings. I still have feelings. I brood over this phrase all day.

•

My life can be divided into thirds: my childhood before I killed my father; my youth and my adult life as a murderer;

then my peaceful life after I stopped murdering. Eunhui symbolizes the last third of my life. Maybe the best way to put it is that she's a kind of amulet for me. As long as I can see Eunhui when I wake up, I won't return to the past where I wandered around looking for victims.

On TV I saw that there was a tiger in a Thailand zoo who'd become deeply depressed after losing her cubs. She didn't eat or move. The zookeeper, unable to stand it any longer, tried to find a way to rouse the tiger. He put a baby pig in the tiger's cage. The tiger took the baby pig for its own and nursed and raised it. Maybe that describes my relationship with Eunhui.

•

I've lost all appetite. If I eat, I throw up. I want to eat something, but I don't know what. I don't want to do anything. I never drank or smoked my whole life, but I feel the urge now. Still, I don't think I'll ever start.

•

"I'm seeing someone," Eunhui told me.

According to what I remember—though of course that's become hard to trust—it's the first time Eunhui has brought up a man. I suddenly realized that I wasn't the least bit prepared to accept him. I'd never imagined Eunhui living with another man. I can't imagine it even now. Could I have actually assumed that she would always live with me?

When Eunhui was in middle school, some guys interested in her used to hang around near the house. They were young and I was already old by then, but there wasn't a single guy who didn't run when he saw me. I didn't try to scare them; all I did was quietly say a few words, but for some reason every one of them became scared and fled. No matter how fierce a dog is, it always surprises its owner when, at the vet's, it tucks its tail between its legs and whimpers. Teenage boys are no different from dogs. From the first confrontation, the look in your eyes determines the relationship.

"So?" I said.

"I'd like you to meet him." Her cheeks flushed.

"So you're going to bring him home?"

"Yes."

"What for?"

"Because you should meet him."

"What for?"

"He wants to marry me."

"Then marry him."

"Please don't be like this."

"Everyone is alone in the end."

"Why bother living if we're going to die anyway?" Her low voice was frosty with anger.

"You've got a point."

"Do you want me to stay unmarried and live with you my entire life, Dad?"

Was that what I wanted? I couldn't say for sure. Because I didn't know, I just wanted to avoid the subject.

"Anyhow, I don't want to meet him," I said. "If you want to marry him, get on with it without me."

"Let's talk about this later."

Eunhui left the room. For some reason I felt ashamed, and angry, too. But I didn't know why. I felt hungry, so I made some noodles. After a few bites, I realized that they tasted weird. Too late it came to me: I left out the soy sauce. I looked everywhere but couldn't find it. I made a note to buy another one. Maybe they'll find dozens of open soy sauce bottles around the house after I die.

I was washing the dishes when my heart sank and I was thrown off again. There was a bowl of unfinished noodles in the sink. Two bowls of noodles already for today's meal.

•

"On my honor, friend," answered Zarathustra, "there is nothing of this that you speak: there is no devil and no hell. Your soul will be dead even sooner than your body; therefore, fear nothing more!"

It's as if Nietzsche had written that for me.

•

One bad thing about living so many years as a murderer: you have no close friends to talk to. But do other people actually have such friends?

•

As soon as thunder and lightning struck outside, the bamboo forest stirred with noise. I didn't sleep all night, I was so intensely irritated by the sound of rain running down the house's eaves. But I used to enjoy that sound.

•

Eunhui brought the man she's seeing to our house. It's the first time she's done this, and she acts serious and grave. I'm forced to accept it. My hands are clammy.

The man came in a four-wheel-drive jeep. I could tell right away it was made for hunting. As if the searchlights installed on the roof weren't enough, three more fog lights were mounted on the bumper. These kinds of cars are revamped so the trunk can be cleaned with water, with two extra car batteries thrown in. When it's hunting season, bastards like him gather in the mountains behind the village.

"I'm Pak Jutae. Pleased to meet you." The man made a full bow, his knees to the floor.

I accepted it with a slight bow. At around five foot six, Pak was on the short side, but he had fair skin and a good build. On second glance, though, he had a narrow forehead, small eyes, and a pointy jaw—a typical rat-like face. He had on thick-rimmed glasses, maybe to hide his face. He seemed both familiar and not, but I couldn't bring it up since I didn't trust my memory at all these days. After he finished bowing, he sat down on his knees. Eunhui sat between us.

I said, "No need to kneel."

"I'm fine, thank you."

I burst out, "I've got dementia. Alzheimer's."

Eunhui's gaze darted up at me. A stare of protest.

I added, "Did Eunhui tell you about it?"

"Yes, she did."

"Even if I forget who you are, please don't take it personally. The doctor says that the most recent memories go first."

"I hear there are good medications these days," Pak said.

"How good can they be?"

Eunhui brought out some sliced pears and apples. While we ate the fruit, Pak slipped easily into telling me a bit about himself.

"I work in real estate," he said.

"Real estate."

"I buy land, divide it into plots, then resell them."

"The work must keep you moving around, looking at land."

"I do have to make an effort to go and see for myself. Land is like women—you can't trust what you hear without seeing for yourself."

I asked, "Any chance we've met before?"

"No, we haven't. Today's the first time." He smiled lightly as he looked up at me.

Eunhui interrupted. "You may have seen Jutae somewhere. He's often in the area these days."

He chimed in, "It's a small town."

I said, "You don't sound like you're from around here."

He had a trace of an accent from down south. He nodded in agreement, but his response wasn't what I'd expected.

He said, "You're right. I was born and raised in Seoul."

"If you marry Eunhui, will you move to Seoul?"

He glanced quickly at Eunhui and back to me, then said no. "Eunhui won't be going anywhere. Why would we leave when you're based here?"

Eunhui said, "We're planning to live downtown."

Her hand reached out and brushed against his, but he didn't take her hand. His hands curled inward like a threatened snail, so Eunhui's hand returned awkwardly to its owner. It happened in the blink of an eye, but it worried me.

When he got up, Eunhui followed him. She slid easily into the hunting-style jeep. It was clear that she'd been in it many times. She rolled the window down and, after telling me she'd be downtown for a bit, rolled it up again.

I went back to the house, closed the door, and started writing about my first meeting with this Pak Jutae before I forgot.

Something didn't feel right. I'd just met the guy, but I already hated him. Why? Had I seen something in him? What was it?

•

My heating bill is too high. The cost of living for everything is skyrocketing.

•

I was shocked when I flipped through my notebook. The bastard was *that* bastard. How was this possible? I feel possessed by a ghost. The guy had calmly walked into my house. As Eunhui's fiancé, at that. And I hadn't even recognized him. Did he think I was acting? Or did he believe that I'd actually forgotten him?

•

I'm reading a book when a note falls out of it. It's yellowed, which means I'd probably written down the quote a long time ago:

"And if you gaze long into an abyss, the abyss will also gaze into you." — Nietzsche

•

Mid-breakfast, I asked Eunhui, "How did you meet this Pak Jutae?"

She said, "By chance. It was truly by chance."

Wisdom begins when people stop believing in the phrase "by chance," which they use out of habit.

•

Sometimes murder is the neatest solution. But not always.

•

That's right. The phone number Pak gave me. The number the bastard wrote down himself. Where did I put it?

I look for it all day but can't find the memo with his number. I comb through the house but find nothing. It's getting harder and harder to find things. Had Eunhui secretly thrown it out?

•

The lady at the local corner store laughed at me and said, "Your shoes are on backwards."

It took me a long time to understand what she meant. What does it mean, wearing your shoes backwards? Is it a figure of speech?

•

After Eunhui left for work, I found a nursing home brochure on her desk.

The ad copy was colorful and enticing, from "A Refuge for the Body and Mind" to "Hotel Facilities." Would my mind and body really find rest there? I put the brochure back on the desk. Eunhui is dreaming of marrying the man she loves and building a home together . . . Shipping me off—the obstacle—to a retirement home . . . Were these Eunhui's ideas, or Pak's schemes?

•

I found his phone number on Eunhui's cell phone. I went shopping downtown, and after buying something, I asked the male clerk for help. One good thing about being old is that people assume you're harmless. The clerk did as I'd asked and, pretending he was a deliveryman, called Pak Jutae.

The clerk explained, "I'm calling because the address on the invoice is too blurry."

It looked like Pak was simply giving out his address without suspicion. After writing it down, the clerk handed it to me.

Errand completed, the clerk beamed at me and asked, "So what happened?"

I said, "My granddaughter ran away from home."

The clerk laughed. Why was he laughing? Does it mean he understands? Or is he mocking me?

•

I began tailing Pak. He spends most of his days at home, then takes the jeep out at four or five p.m. He rarely goes to places like teahouses. Sometimes he stands in someone's field or fruit orchard and looks around. It's as if he's in real estate and sizing up property, but then he doesn't meet enough people for that line of work. Sometimes he goes out late at night and speeds along without a clear destination. My instincts tell me that he might not be hunting animals. If my guess is right, would this be God's idea of a classy joke? Or God's judgment?

•

I contemplated turning Pak in to the police. What did they call it, the thing the courts give out? That's right, a warrant. They need it to search the bastard's house and car. But if they search and don't find concrete evidence, they'll release him. Then he'll suspect me—he's already wary and keeping an eye on me—and if the bastard is really a killer, Eunhui or I would be his next target. I see us through his eyes. A seventy-year-old man with Alzheimer's and a fragile woman in her twenties living in isolation near a mountain. We must look like easy prey.

•

I sat Eunhui down and told her about Pak Jutae. What I'd seen in his trunk when I'd rear-ended his jeep. How bright and fresh the blood had been. How he had fled. After that, how long he had kept his eye on me. If such a man ends up in front of her "by chance," what that "chance" meant, and how much danger she was in.

Eunhui listened patiently, then said, "Dad, I truly have no idea what you're talking about."

I tried again, but she reacted the same way. She said I was speaking so incoherently that she couldn't understand me. I felt the way I had when I'd first learned English and rambled on in front of an American. I did my very best to speak, the other person tried hard to understand, but nothing got communicated. Eunhui only took in the fact that I intensely disliked her man. I said, "It's not that I hate him; I'm warning you that you're in danger. You're dating an extremely dangerous man. Your meeting him was definitely not chance."

Our talk ultimately fails. Eunhui's patience runs out, and as I become more impatient, I become even more inarticulate. As usual, language is slower than action, unclear and ambiguous. When now is the time to act.

I hear the sound of Eunhui's muffled weeping from her room.

•

I cautiously tracked down a phone booth without surveillance cameras nearby, and from there called 112 to report Pak.

I muffled the receiver with a cloth and disguised my voice. I told the police that Pak Jutae with his hunting-style jeep could be the serial killer they were looking for. At first, the operator didn't understand me.

I tried to slowly, clearly describe Pak's jeep. This time the operator seemed to get it, but did not take me very seriously. He asked me to identify myself. I said I couldn't—I was worried about my safety. He asked me why I thought Pak Jutae was the killer. I answered, "You should have the car examined. I saw blood coming out of it."

•

I definitely entered the room to do something, but since I can't for the life of me remember what that something is, I stand around absent-mindedly for a while. It's as if the God who'd been masterminding me had let go of the controls. I stand there blankly, not knowing what to do. What happens if I forget like this again just as I catch Pak?

•

The news says that a suspected serial killer had been held and interrogated by the police, then released without charge. Why had the police let Pak go? Had they really not found anything? Times have changed, but they've remained incompetent.

Will I have to deal with him myself? Is there really no other way?

•

For the first time in my life, I began considering murder out of necessity. If a man whose hobby was collecting high-end audio gear had to buy an amp for a work event, he would probably feel the way I did.

•

I've decided on a final goal before I die. To kill Pak Jutae. Before I forget who he is.

•

I once heard about an American struck by lightning who became a musical genius overnight. He began playing the piano though he'd never had lessons, manically composed music, and later became an orchestra conductor. As for me, after damaging my head in a car accident, I lost all interest in murder and ended up becoming like everyone else. I lived like that for over twenty years, but now I'm preparing for a murder, not because I want to but because I have to. God is commanding me to make banal my sacred misdeeds.

•

The doctor said that dementia patients struggle with multitasking. If you put a teapot on the gas range and then start doing something else, nine out of ten times you'll end up burning the pot. He said that even washing dishes and doing laundry at the same time could become difficult. For women, one of the first activities they have to give up is cooking. Cooking, surprisingly, requires a systematic completion of several tasks at the same time.

The doctor advised, "It's best to simplify every aspect of your life and develop the habit of doing one thing at a time."

I decided to follow the doctor's advice. For the time being, I have to focus with all that's left of my abilities. The bastard can't be taken lightly. He's young, strong, and armed. He's also a good talker who's charmed Eunhui into marriage in no time. He'll have two goals for approaching her. The first, to get a better look at me. The second, to kill her. If he needs to, he'll probably wipe me out, too. But the bastard already knows that I have Alzheimer's. If he decides he doesn't need to kill me, he won't overextend himself. It's Eunhui he's lusting for, not me. I have to get rid of him before that happens. The news reports make me think that the bastard kidnaps young women, brutally tortures them, and kills them.

After twenty-five years, I've returned to the work I am best at. But now I'm too old for it. One improvement on the past is that I no longer need to secure an escape route. You could say that the sum of hunting is in the pursuit and capture. In contrast, what's most important in murder isn't to seize the desired object, but to safely escape. It's important to catch, but you can't be caught yourself. This time will be different. I'm going to give everything I have to catch the bastard. This time the goal isn't murder, but the hunt.

When hunting, the first step is to find the prey's territory. Second is to scout a good location and stake it out. Third, not to miss a single chance to capture it. If you fail, return to step one.

•

Now that I have decided to catch Pak Jutae, my appetite has suddenly returned. I sleep well and feel good. I'm starting to get confused about whether I'm doing it for Eunhui's sake or for mine.

•

Pak lives on the first and basement floors of a two-story house. If you follow a small field to the back, it leads to a building that used to be a cowshed. The jeep's nose is rammed into the back of the shed, and its rear juts out. Without pushing the door open and walking into the yard, it's hard to see anything. A cleverly placed barrier of bush clover almost perfectly blocks the house from view. This kind of house may protect your privacy, but it's fatally weak against trespassers, because if someone breaks in, it's impossible to know what's happening inside. So that means Pak is fearless about outside enemies. The house quietly betrays his thoughts: I can take care of my own property. The only thing I care about is staying out of sight.

A granny well over seventy lives on the second floor. What is her connection to Pak? Was she renting, or were they related? In any case, she probably wouldn't get in the way. She has a stoop and has trouble moving.

I'm tired. I'm calling it a day.

•

Eunhui was getting ready for work when I saw that her neck was bruised. It's the kind of mark left after someone's choked you. I ask Eunhui about it. She automatically pulls in her neck as if trying to get rid of it altogether. I press on and ask her if that Pak bastard did this to her.

She says, "Please don't call anyone you want a bastard, Dad."

"Then what happened to your neck?"

Eunhui tells me that I went into her bedroom and tried to choke her. I can't believe her and I can't not believe her. Everything about me is like this now.

"Why did you do it?" she says. "Dad, you're not that kind of person. It was like you went insane. You nearly killed me."

"A lie. You're lying."

"Why would I lie? Please, please accept the facts. Dad, you've got Alzheimer's!"

Eunhui throws the word "Alzheimer's" at me like a hammer. I suddenly feel drained. I have no memory of it, not even as vague traces of a dream. I feel lost. If I'd really done this to her, it's a miracle she is still alive, since I have powerful arms. I beg Eunhui to forgive me. I also tell her to always lock her door before bed. After blowing her nose and wiping her tears, she snatches the nursing home pamphlet I'd seen the other day from a drawer. I ignore it, but she doesn't give in.

"Dad, it's too much for me. And for your sake, you should be at the home anyway. What if something happens when I'm not here?"

I understand. Who wants to die choking in their sleep?

"All right," I say. "I'll take a look."

According to the law, Eunhui can have me locked up in a mental hospital without my consent. If you make a call, an ambulance arrives and stocky men put you in a straitjacket and throw you in an isolation ward. That's it. Unless the family gives permission for your release, you can be locked up forever. I'd heard of cases in which family members, unhappy with their inheritance, banded together, forced their drunk father into a mental hospital, and started negotiating. I'd already been diagnosed with Alzheimer's, so Eunhui could easily get rid of me. Right this minute if she wanted to.

A nursing home would be better than a mental hospital, but I don't want to go anywhere just yet. Either way, I don't have much time left as a free man.

"Let's go for a visit." Eunhui spoke fervently as she held my hand. "Just have a look, that's all."

I gave in and agreed. Only after Eunhui left for work, I remembered: I had choked Eunhui's mother to death.

•

I bought a voice recorder people use to study languages and hung it around my neck by a cord. No matter how simple the task, I record it before I do something. Afterward, I do it. Midway, if I forget what I'm doing, I press Replay. I'll listen to what I've just recorded and try it again.

I say, "I'll go to the bathroom and pee," then go to the bathroom. I say, "I'm going to boil water and make coffee," and go boil the water. The person I was a few minutes ago gives orders to the person I'll be a few minutes later. Like this, the person I am is endlessly divided. Even when I'm zoning out, I'll see the recorder and automatically press the Replay button. I'm not in desperate need of it yet, but I'm preparing for the worst. I have to tirelessly repeat for my body to remember.

•

I tried talking to Eunhui again, but she just cried quietly as I spoke. Why was she crying? All I did was warn her of the danger she was in, so why does she look so aggrieved? I was only worried about her. I have no way of understanding such complex emotions. Was it sadness, or anger, or grief? I couldn't tell. Her eyes wet with tears, she pleaded, "Please don't talk that way about Jutae anymore. It hurts to listen to it. He's a good man. Calling the man I'm to marry a serial killer— aren't you taking it too far? How can you suspect a person like that without evidence?" In any case, she finally fully comprehends my point. That alone is a relief. At least I've succeeded in planting doubt about the bastard in her heart. What destroyed the ever-victorious Othello was Iago's seed of doubt.

"You're not even my real father!" she said again, and fled to her room. She's right, but I feel gravely insulted.

•

I'm lying down when I hear footsteps coming toward my house. Five young folks in uniform. At first I thought they were the police.

"Hello," they said. There were three men, two women. I asked who they were, and they said they were students from the Police Academy.

I invited them inside and asked, "What's this about?"

They said they were in the middle of a group project. Their assignment was to select and investigate old unsolved cases. They showed me a few articles they had photocopied. They were all about murders I'd committed. It was kind of amazing to me that events from decades ago still came back so vividly.

One of them said, "Our group suspects that these murders are connected—the work of a serial killer. Though no one thought of it that way back then."

The police cadets rattled on excitedly. The girls were pretty and the boys, handsome. Even in the middle of discussing serial murder, they would burst out laughing for no reason. These kids, they think playing FBI is fun.

I said, "I've got no idea what you're talking about. Why have you showed up at my house making a racket?"

Instead of an answer, a new character appeared as if out of

a scene in a play. A man around his mid-fifties. The students stood up and saluted him.

He said, "It's all right. Sit down."

The new character was Detective Ahn. He introduced himself and handed me his business card. He said he couldn't just send the students out alone, so he had accompanied them. He sat behind them, appearing indifferent, but his gaze cast about the corners of the house out of professional habit.

When he said, "Carry on," the students became more insistent, their faces newly flushed with determination.

One said, "We drew lines connecting the locations of these cases. Here, please have a look."

The lines they'd made on the map formed an octagon, and the village I lived in was at the center. A female student with a small face and a high-bridged nose, her eyes shining with excitement, shoved the map at me.

She said, "We believe that if the criminal exists, he'd be in this area . . ."

My neighborhood.

". . . based on what we've deduced. Though of course there's no chance he'd still be living here."

A hasty conclusion. Detective Ahn, who'd been drowsing, suddenly straightened and frowned at the students.

I murmured, "In our neighborhood."

"Sir, you've lived here the whole time, so we wondered if you ever saw anyone suspicious back then."

I said, "Back then, there were a lot of spies. Since the neighborhood's close to the North, a lot of them did come over. If a friend we spent time with disappeared for a few days, we'd say, 'Uncle must have come.' Uncle from the North, we meant. No one said as much, but everyone knew what was going on.

Outsiders hiking in the area were often stopped and interrogated as potential spies."

A tall male student became impatient and interrupted. "We're not looking for spies."

I raised my hand and stopped him. "What I'm saying is that if someone looked suspicious, they would've already been arrested twice over. I mean, people became rich overnight back then by turning spies in and collecting the reward money."

The lanky male student said, "So you're saying that the criminal would be one of those arrested as a spy and then released. But how do we find out?"

I said, "Maybe the local precinct still has those records."

From the back, Detective Ahn cut in. "They don't."

"They don't?" a slender-faced girl said with reproach. These confident young Police Academy students, these kids who had watched TV shows like *CSI* and dreamed of joining the force, would dismiss a provincial homicide detective in a second—but if you had all been there, if you'd been the cops in my district, would you have caught me? The records were probably a pitiful mess. A careless prelim investigation. Little mutual cooperation. The few suspects they managed to round up released with verdicts of not guilty. I'd read that a couple of them sued the government, claiming they were tortured during interrogation, and they eventually won reparations once Korea became a democracy.

Detective Ahn said, "Do you know what the eighties were like? Even police in the Gangwon-do countryside wore helmets, and cops were attacked with Molotov cocktails in front of universities in Seoul. You think anyone cared that some people died out in the country?"

Detective Ahn went out for a smoke. The students followed him. While the rest of them were putting on their shoes, one male student whispered to me, "Detective Ahn was in charge of a few of those cases. He's been known to work weekends to catch the murderer, even now, though the statute of limitations has passed. There must be a reason he can't let it go."

A girl standing in the yard added, "You've got to be careful with country people. They're more stubborn than they look."

The kids don't know what they're talking about. That's why I like them.

Detective Ahn stopped smoking and, as if he'd suddenly had an idea, came back to the veranda.

"Do you have any family?" he asked.

"I've got a daughter."

"I see . . ."

A man who'd lived alone for a long time. He's probably looking for a lone wolf. The students began scouring the neighborhood, but Ahn didn't follow them. Instead, he perched on the edge of the veranda.

He said, "I shouldn't be saying this in front of you, but now that I'm getting older, I'm breaking down everywhere." He tapped his knees.

If someone saw us, he would think that Detective Ahn and I were old friends from the village.

"Are you ill?" I asked.

"Diabetes, arthritis, high blood pressure. There isn't anything I don't have. It's all because of these stakeouts for the same guy. I'm sick of it."

"Why don't you retire somewhere peaceful?"

51

"I'll get my rest eventually, when I'm in the grave."

"Naturally. The grave's most comfortable."

We were quiet for a moment.

The detective said, "Doesn't everyone have that one thing? The thing they have to see to completion before they die?"

"Of course they do," I agreed. "I've got one, too."

"What is it?"

"Nothing much to share. One of the students mentioned how you're still trying to catch the criminal. What will you get out of it even if you catch him? You can't put him behind bars anymore."

"I don't know why I keep returning to those cases. I'm getting worse about it these days. At the least, I need to let the killer know that someone hasn't forgotten and is still after him. That way he can't sleep easy."

So, Detective Ahn, you know what murder is. What a crime scene soaked in blood is like. Murder and its irreversible power. There's something in it that captivates us and pulls us in. But Detective Ahn, I always sleep well.

I said, "Anyway, you should really watch your health. These days I keep forgetting everything."

"But you look fit for your age."

"You know how old I am?"

I sensed him flinch. I pretended not to notice and changed the subject.

"The doctor says my brain's withering. Later, it'll be just like a dried-up walnut."

Ahn stayed quiet.

I added, "By tomorrow, I might forget you paid me a visit."

•

The students leave, but I stay pumped up. I wanted to sit them down and tell all. Walk them through from the first murder to the last, every single one of them still vivid to me. They'd be rapt listeners. Kids, there's no main subject in the documents you're looking at, only lines of objects and predicates. If you replace the name "John Doe" on the line, I'd be that very name, that subject. I was dying to reveal myself to them, but managed to hold back. I still had one thing left to do.

•

I had to make a trip downtown. When I got back, I could tell that someone had entered the house while I was gone. The person had been careful, but someone had definitely gone through the house. There were some things missing, no matter how much I hunted for them. They'd been taken, for sure. Was it a burglar? I'd never been robbed before.

When Eunhui returned from work, I told her that we'd had a burglar. She looked at me with pity and said no such thing had happened. She asked me what had gone missing, but I couldn't remember. Still, something was definitely missing. I sensed it. But I couldn't form the words for it.

"People say all dementia patients are like that," she said. "They think their daughter-in-law or nurse is a thief."

They call it "theft delusion." I know that much. But this isn't delusion. Things have definitely disappeared. I always keep my journal and my voice recorder on me, so they were spared, but something else was missing.

"I know," I said. "The dog has disappeared. The dog's disappeared."

"Dad, when did we ever have a dog?"

Strange. I was sure we had a dog.

•

The cherry blossoms along the main road into my hometown were lovely. In the spring, people strolled in long lines through the tunnel of cherry blossom trees, first planted under Japanese rule. When the flowers were in full bloom, I'd take a detour around that road on purpose. It scared me to stare too long at them. You can chase away a fierce dog with a stick, but you can't do that with flowers. Flowers are fierce. That street of cherry blossoms—I keep thinking about it. What had scared me so much? They were just flowers.

•

I've never once been arrested or detained, but prison was always in my thoughts. In my confused dreams, I'm always walking down a jail corridor that I've actually never once entered. I search for my assigned cell and am bewildered when I can't find it. Or sometimes I'm assigned a cell already crammed full of people, and when I enter, all the people I've killed smile brightly at me, waiting.

I always recall the prisons I've seen on TV or read about in novels as worlds of iron. The iron cell doors clanging open. Barbed wire decorating the towering walls like vines. Handcuffs and iron shackles tight around the wrists. The clinking of the prisoners' plates and trays. Even their gray uniforms remind me of iron.

Each person has a different image of salvation. It might look like an English garden with sunlight beaming down on the lawn, or a traditional Swiss cottage, its sills lined with flowers. For me, I've always imagined it as a prison. I see rough men reeking of sweat from their armpits, groins, their entire bodies. Only inside that prison, I'd be tamed within the strict hierarchy of convicts and utterly forget who I am. It'll feel like I'm finally able to put my restless self to sleep.

I also fantasize about solitary confinement. I repeatedly imagine being trapped in a coffin-sized room, my hands bound behind me as I lick my plate with my tongue. I'm miserably trampled and drained, suffering from an intense longing for the earth beneath my feet, the world that I've left behind. Imagining this gives me intense pleasure. I'm probably exhausted from making every single decision and executing them by myself for too long. A world that shrinks the autonomy of my demonic self to zero; for me, that place is prison and solitary confinement. A place where I can't just kill anyone and bury him, a place where I wouldn't dare to think those thoughts, a place where my body and mind would be completely destroyed. A place where I would lose myself forever.

•

The public stadium. I remember the crowds swarming in. At the rally, they said that the North had sent down guerrilla units, captured American warships, shot the first lady. Public speakers roared: *Let's rip up the Red pig Kim Il-sung and slaughter him. Let's beat up the Communists.* Kids sat in the front and gazed up reverently at the platform. We knew what was about to happen. We were anticipating the government-sponsored spectacle of erupting blood, the severing of body parts.

"It's him!" A friend pointed at a young man sitting behind the platform. "Today it's that man. I'm sure of it."

"How can you tell?"

"'Cause he's a gangster!"

He did immediately stand out. Aside from him, the rest were community leaders: the mayor, the chief of police, the general running the military district, the superintendent of education, and the school principals. Only the young man radiated tension—tension typical of a life dependent on brute strength. He was so broad-chested that his suit jacket wouldn't button up all the way.

Moments later, he got up on the platform to great applause. The rally was reaching its climax. Some overexcited women cried and fainted. As soon as the man appeared, two women in cotton dresses walked in front of him with a scroll of paper. He screamed, "Those fucking Commies, those fuckers, let's wipe them off the planet!" Then he pulled out a knife. The women screamed and covered their eyes. He immediately swung the knife downward and sliced off his pinkie.

"ERADICATE THE COMMUNISTS!"

The two women took that pledge of his, written in blood, and held it up from either side, high in the air. Immediately the stadium echoed with the military band's performance of "The Torch of the Red Hunt": *We who protect these beautiful rivers and mountains, we live with the spirit of men. We risk fields of fiery mortar to protect our families back home. Fellow soldiers, I'll protect my country. Under the torch of the Red Hunt, I'll risk my life.*

Medical aides rush out of the ambulance parked beside the stadium. The man shouts, "I don't need it. I don't need anything!" The young gangster is agitated at the sight of his own blood. Like a cornered animal, he whirls around, gasping for air. Only when the chief of police comes and whispers in his ear does he finally shrink back. The medics help him down and begin to stanch the bleeding.

Gangsters got up on the platform at every rally and cut their finger off as they screamed, "Crush the Communists!" The rally truly ended only when blood splattered on the platform. Rumor had it that the police force requested gang cooperation each time, for dramatic effect. Their boss would single out his underlings for the task. I wondered, Did our country have enough gang members to handle the many public rallies? But one day these rallies suddenly disappeared, after our president was shot and killed by the secretary of state.

While everyone was trying to catch the phantom that was communism, I was doing my own hunting. An official announcement about a man I killed in 1976 declared that an armed spy had murdered the man: "We believe that the criminal brutally slaughtered his victim, then fled back to the North. Based on the savage nature of the crime, it is clear that the puppet regime of the North was responsible."

Since the murder was apparently committed by a nonexistent ghost, there was no need to catch the criminal.

•

Returning home from downtown, I ran into a stranger at the edge of the village. The young man stared directly into my eyes, his arms crossed. Who was he? Why was he being so openly hostile to me? I was terrified. Out of habit, I first assumed he was a police detective. But I went home, searched my notes, and realized who he was. It was that bastard Pak Jutae.

Why was his face still not imprinted in my memory? I was

frustrated. Anyway, I write it down before I forget. About how he showed up again.

•

Eunhui brought up the nursing home again. She said, Let's at least have a look. I had become curious about how old people with dementia live, so I decided to go. But Eunhui only ended up getting angry. I asked her why she was angry, and she claimed that I'd said, "When did I say I'd go?" and started resisting.

"I did? I don't remember . . ."

Eunhui entreated me again, so I immediately followed her. Later, when I reviewed what I'd recorded, I heard myself in the car repeatedly asking her, "Where are we going?"

Each time she answered patiently, "Dad, you said you wanted to go see the nursing home, so that's what we're doing right now. We're just going to look."

Eunhui took pictures of the home, saying it would help me remember it later. I used my recorder and took notes.

The elderly residents looked at peace. I sat for a bit with a group of old folks playing board games. They welcomed me. A game of building blocks wasn't going smoothly. The pieces kept tumbling, but they were enjoying themselves.

Eunhui said, "Look at them. Everyone's having a good time."

She doesn't know that there's no room for others in the happiness I'd pursued. I don't remember ever feeling happy while doing something with others. I had always turned deep inside myself, and in there I discovered a lasting pleasure. Like a pet snake that requires hamsters, the monster in me required constant feeding. Only at those times did others have any meaning.

I felt disgusted as soon as the old people began wildly clapping and laughing. Laughter equals weakness. It means offering yourself unarmed to others. It's a sign that you're willing to turn yourself into bait. These people had no power—they were coarse and childish.

We also stopped by a lounge full of chatting residents. Their conversations were disjointed fragments. One with severe dementia kept talking nonsense to himself, and those listening to him blabbered back. Nothing they said was very funny, but they kept exploding with laughter.

Eunhui said to the social welfare officer taking us around, "How do they understand each other and keep up conversations like that?"

As if it wasn't the first time the woman had heard this question, she said, "Drunk people still enjoy each other's company, for example. Full mental faculties aren't necessarily essential to enjoy talking to one another."

•

My notepad has the random phrase "future memories" jotted on it. What had I seen when I wrote this down? It is definitely my handwriting, but no matter how much I study it, it means nothing to me. Isn't the word called "memory" because it happened in the past? But the phrase "future memories" . . . Frustrated, I looked it up on the internet and found that "future memories" means remembering what you have to do in the future. These were the memories that dementia patients were said to lose first. "Take pills thirty minutes after eating" is an

59

example of a future memory. If you lose your past memories, you forget who you are, and if you lose your future memories, you end up living eternally in the present. But without a past and a future, does the present have any meaning? Still, what can you do? If the rails are broken, the train has to stop.

Anyway, I'm worried about the important work ahead.

•

I like a quiet world. I can't live in a city because too many noises rush in at me. Too many signs, billboards, and people and their facial expressions. I can't interpret all of that. It scares me.

•

I went to a writers' reunion for the first time in ages. The area's literary folk have aged a lot. One person who'd passionately written novels is now studying genealogy. It means his heart is starting to move toward the dead. Some who'd written poetry are now obsessed with calligraphy, also an art that belongs to the dead.

One old man says, "Now that I'm older, I enjoy reading other people's writing."

Another old man agrees, adding, "One of the original principles of Asian art is imitation."

Now old, they return to the East. There's a retired vocational school principal whom everyone still calls Principal Park. He asks me if I've continued to write poetry.

I say, "Sure."

He asks me to show him some.

"They're not worth showing anyone."

"Still, I'm impressed. Writing poems after all this time."

"Meaning, I'm trying to write poems, but it's not going well. Maybe it's age."

"What are they about?" Principal Park asks.

"What I always wrote about, really."

"Still the same old subjects—blood, corpses? You should mellow with age, old man."

"I have mellowed out. Anyway, I'd really like to write at least one good poem before I go."

"If there's something you want to do, don't put it off. Just do it. Who knows if you'll be around tomorrow?"

"Exactly."

We drank our coffee. I say, "I'm rereading the classics these days. Greek classics."

"Which ones?"

"Tragedies, epics, the like. I read *Oedipus Rex* and the *Odyssey.*"

"Those kinds of books interest you?" Principal Park asks as he fiddles with his reading glasses.

"I've found there are things you only see when you're old."

I went to the bathroom and checked my recorder. Everything had recorded well.

•

I found a good poem on my bookshelf. I was excited and read and reread the poem, trying to memorize it. Then I realized that I'd written the poem.

•

My journal shocked me once again. The Police Academy students' visit had been cleanly erased from my brain. I now experience this often, but never get used to it. It's different from forgetting, since it feels as if it had never happened in the first place. It's more like reading a page from an Antarctic explorer's log or a crime novel. But the handwriting is definitely mine. I have absolutely no memory of it, but I write it down once again: *Yesterday, five Police Academy cadets and someone named Detective Ahn paid me a visit.*

These days, I only remember things vividly from the distant past.

My very first memory: sitting in a basin and splashing water in the middle of the yard. I was probably taking a bath. Since I was small enough to fit in the basin, I was likely three years old then, or younger. Some woman's face was close enough to be touching mine. Probably my mother. There were other women coming and going in the background. My mother briskly scrubbed at my body, turning me this way and that, as if I were an octopus she'd bought at the fish market. I vividly remember the moment I felt her breath against my neck, and how I frowned as sunlight pierced my eyes. Since I don't remember my sister being there, either she wasn't born yet or she was elsewhere. Just as my bath ended, my mother grabbed my penis and said something, but I don't remember anything after that. Except I remember thinking: That's strange, she pulled my penis, but why does my butt hurt? Then, last, the raucous cackling of women.

Man is a prisoner of time. A dementia patient is someone trapped in a cell where the walls are collapsing inward. They're moving faster and faster.

I can't breathe.

•

The more I think about it, the visit from the Police Academy cadets makes me uneasy. Won't they get in the way of my catching Pak Jutae?

•

Eunhui didn't come home last night. I imagined the worst and prepared myself. I made my decision and got ready to find the bastard as soon as daylight hit. Then sleep overwhelmed me. When I woke up, I saw that Eunhui must have stopped by, then left again. It was noon.

Was she acting out?

•

When I skim through my journal or listen to what I've recorded, I discover events there I have no memory of. It's natural, since I'm losing my memory, but it's weird reading about your actions, thoughts, and speech as you lose them. It's like rereading a Russian novel that you read a long time ago. The setting is familiar, and so are the characters. But it's all somehow new. I keep asking myself, Did it really happen?

•

I asked Eunhui why she hadn't come home the night before. She avoided looking at me and kept tucking her hair behind her ears. She does this whenever I say something she doesn't want to hear. I see the younger Eunhui beneath that habitual gesture, that immature, naïve kid who once depended on me.

Eunhui tried to change the subject, and said, "The past is the past."

"Why're you suddenly acting out?" I asked. "Where were you last night?"

"So what if I stayed out?" Eunhui talked back, nothing like herself.

Her flaring up means she'd definitely been with that bastard. She no longer bothers to make up excuses; she thinks I'll forget anyway. She doesn't know how desperately I'm trying to hold on to my memories.

"The bastard's a bluebeard."

"A bluebeard? He doesn't have a beard."

Eunhui lacks refinement.

•

Why's the bastard letting Eunhui live? Is it his way of holding her hostage? Is he keeping her near him so I can't turn him in? If so, he could just get rid of me first. What are you waiting for, Pak Jutae?

•

Eunhui's on the phone with a friend. I crouch down, my ear to the door, and listen in. She's fallen in love with Pak. She can't stop talking about him. She goes on about what a wonderful person he is, how good he is to her. For the first time, I feel like I'm listening to the undiluted voice of a woman in love. Eunhui's never lived in a typical family, since she lost her parents when she was young, then lived with me ever since. For the first time, Eunhui is lost in fantasies of having her own family. But Eunhui, why that bastard, of all men? Why, of all people, is the bastard you love fated to die at the hands of the same man who killed your parents?

•

I want to kill Pak Jutae, and soon. But I keep losing track of my mind. I feel impatient. If I keep on like this, will I end up a man unable to do anything at all? I feel depressed.

•

I found Detective Ahn's business card in Eunhui's wallet. Why is he pursuing me? To realize his final goal in life?

•

Eunhui has begun outright avoiding me ever since I'd warned her about Pak, but I'm trying not to feel disappointed in her. Someday when my brain is shriveled up and I can't remember anything, when I become totally helpless, or even when I'm dead and buried, Eunhui will, I hope, discover my journal. She'll hear my recordings. Then she'll learn about what kind of person I was. She'll know what I had planned to do for her sake.

•

Eunhui said, "A policeman visited me at the lab today." When I asked her who it was, Detective Ahn fit her description.

She added, "He asked me about my mother."

"So what did you say?"

"As if I know anything about her! I said I knew nothing."

"Why would a detective come around after all this time, asking about your mother?"

"How would I know? I just told him to tell me if he finds out anything."

"And?"

"He said he would. But something was a little off."

"What?"

"You told me my mother died. But the detective said that she was declared missing. He said, as for my father, the hospital issued a death certificate so he's officially reported dead, but my mother isn't. She was missing for so long that she was finally declared dead. Can you tell me what happened? Something feels wrong."

"You said that to Detective Ahn? That something wasn't right?"

"Yes. He said he agreed."

"It's what the orphanage director told me, that your mother was dead. So of course I always believed this."

"Where do you think she is now?"

"Who knows? She might even be somewhere very nearby."

In our yard, for instance.

•

When I replay the recorder, I discover that I've recently saved several songs on it. I've got songs by Kim Choo Ja and Cho Yong-pil. There's Park In-soo's "Spring Rain" as well: *Spring rain, spring rain, you make me cry. Till when will you keep falling? You make me cry, spring rain.*

Why had I sung these tunes?

I'm not sure anymore.

Because I'm not sure, I get angry. I try to delete them, but I don't know how to, and finally give up.

•

After napping, I woke up and found Pak sitting at my bedside. He pressed firmly down on my forehead so I couldn't get up. He said, "I know who you are." I asked, "What do you mean, you know who I am?" He said that as soon as he'd laid eyes on me, he knew we were the same breed. And that he'd known instantly that I recognized him, too.

I asked, "Are you going to kill me?"

He shook his head. He said he was preparing a more amusing game, then opened the door and left. As expected, my hunch was correct. But what game was he planning?

•

Shame and guilt: Shame is when you're embarrassed for yourself. Guilt lies outside yourself, with others. Some people probably feel guilt but no shame. They fear being punished by others. Me, I feel shame but I don't feel guilt. I've never feared what people think, and I'm not afraid of punishment. Still, my sense of shame is extreme. I've even killed someone solely out of shame—my type of person is the more dangerous kind.

Letting Pak kill Eunhui would be a shameful thing. I'd never forgive myself.

•

Over the years, I've saved many lives. Even if those lives belong to animals that don't speak.

•

When I come to my senses, Detective Ahn is sitting in front of me. I have absolutely no recall of when he came over and sat on the veranda and began talking. He keeps talking. It's like watching a TV show that's already half over.

". . . that store, of all places. So of course I'd go nuts. Would you—"

I cut him off. "What store do you mean?"

"I'm speaking of the cigarette store. The store where I said I always bought cigarettes."

"What about that store?"

Detective Ahn might look like a big bear, but his gaze is at once indifferent and sharp.

"Your memory must really come and go. I said the murdered woman used to work there."

Now I know where this is heading. My eighth victim was someone folks called the "cigarette girl." So Detective Ahn had been a regular there. But how had our conversation led to her?

"And?"

"She still shows up in my dreams, begging me to catch her killer."

I said, "Be sure to catch him."

Detective Ahn said, "I'm going to."

"But isn't getting the serial killer who's on the loose right now more urgent?"

"That's the Special Investigation Bureau's task. As for me, since I'm just holding out till retirement, I'll stick to my hobbies until my time's up."

Detective Ahn retrieved a pack of cigarettes from his pocket and stuck one between his lips, defensively repeating, "These cigarettes, so bad for your health, are supposed to be good for Alzheimer's."

I said, "I should have taken up smoking."

"Would you like a smoke?" he asked, offering me one.

"I don't know how to."

The cigarette smoke slowly rose up one of the veranda's wooden columns.

"Don't say you've never lit up before," Ahn said. "Anyway, your dog seems to like people. What's his name?"

He made a clucking sound to attract the dog. From a fixed, safe distance, the yellow-haired mutt wagged his tail.

"He's not ours," I said. "I should close the front gate or something—everyone keeps coming and going as they please."

"But the dog was here last time, too. He's not yours?"

"I'm telling you, he showed up one day and keeps hanging around. Scram!"

"Leave him alone—he's a tame one. But what's that in his mouth?"

"A cow bone. The neighbor down the road is always making beef-bone soup, so he would've gotten it from there. It smells foul. How can a person live day and night on beef-bone soup alone?" As an afterthought, I added casually, "So, after all this time, why hasn't the criminal you've been pursuing not been hauled in? Maybe it's because he's already dead."

"That's possible. But he wouldn't have lived in peace. Even my sleep is uneasy, so there's no way a guy who's killed so many could sleep like a baby. If he's dead, he would have caught every nasty disease out there first and suffered. Don't they say that stress is the source of all illnesses?"

"Do you think it would influence dementia, too?"

His eyes became alert. "What? Murder?"

I gestured dismissively. "No, I mean stress."

"There's probably some connection."

"What person doesn't have stress? That's life's . . ."

I couldn't remember what was next, so I sat there dumbly. Detective Ahn said carefully, "Tonic?"

"That's it. Isn't it the fuel of life?"

We laughed on and on for no reason. The mutt crouched and barked at us.

•

Everything's starting to get mixed up. I think I've jotted something down, but when I check, there's nothing there. Things I'm sure are on my recorder, I find written down instead. And the opposite happens, too. Memory, records, delusions—I can't separate them anymore. The doctor said I should listen to music. I followed his advice and began listening to classical at home. Who knows if it'll help. He also wrote me a new prescription.

•

Within days, my condition improved. Was it because of the new meds? I felt better and wanted to go out. My confidence returned. My muddled head was clearer, and my memory seemed to be improving. My doctor and Eunhui agreed with me. The doctor explained that dementia often accompanies depression in old age, and that the depression can make the dementia worse. So if you treat the depression, dementia seems to slow its progress or at least temporarily improve.

For the first time in ages, my confidence soars. I feel capable of doing everything. While my mind's alert, I've got to do what I've been putting off.

•

They found another female body. Like the others, it was in a ditch on a country road. The victim's bindings and the location where she was dumped matched the other murders. The police increased the number of checkpoints and now crowd around them like a pack of wild dogs.

•

It suddenly occurred to me: I might be jealous of Pak.

•

Now and then I think, If I'm caught, they can't actually punish me. It's strange. I should be happy about it, but I'm not. Instead, it feels as if I've been abandoned by the human race. I don't know philosophy. There's a beast inside me. A beast doesn't have a moral code. I don't have any morals, but why do I feel this way? Maybe because I'm old. Maybe only luck has kept me from getting caught. But why do I feel so unhappy? And what exactly is happiness? Feeling alive—isn't that happiness? Wasn't I happiest when day after day I was thinking about murder or planning one? Back then I was as taut as a stringed instrument. Then as now, I've lived only for the present. There's been no past and there's no future.

A few years ago at the dentist's, I found a book with the title *Finding Flow: The Psychology of Engagement with Everyday Life* and skimmed through it. The author emphasized the importance of immersion, the joy it brings you. Look here, Mr. Author, when I was young, older people got worried when a kid became obsessed with something. They would call him single-minded. Back then, only the crazy ones had that kind of focus. If you knew how engrossed I was way back when I was killing, and how enjoyable it was, if you knew how dangerous obsession is, you'd shut up. Immersion is dangerous. And therefore, enjoyable.

I don't remember any of the last twenty-five years I've spent not hurting a soul. The boring daily life was followed by more of the same. I've lived far too long as this wrong person.

I want to become obsessed again.

•

After my car accident, I suffered from severe delirium. It was so bad that the nurses bound me to the bedpost. Since my body was tied up, my mind fluttered away. I dreamed a lot. One eerily vivid dream still stays with me as if it had actually happened. In the dream I am a company man and have three kids. The two older ones are daughters, and the youngest is a son. I take the packed lunch my wife made and head to work at what looks like a government building. The sweet boredom of a stable life where everything is known. Not once in my life have I felt this.

After I eat lunch with my colleagues, play a bit of pool, and return to the office, a female colleague tells me that my wife called. On the phone she screamed, "Darling, darling, darling!" And the phone cuts off just as she says, "Please save me!" While speeding home I try to speak but can't. When I open the door, I see my wife and three children laid out in a row. At that moment, the police rush in and handcuff me. "What is this?" I say. "I sped home in order to catch myself?"

Once the delirium passes, I feel bereft whenever I recall the dream. But what had I lost? The brief taste of ordinary life that I'd been exiled from? My wife and kids? Grieving for something that was never mine didn't make sense. It was probably just hallucinations from the anesthetic. So does that mean my brain can't tell the difference? But my relief the moment the dream-police handcuff me is something to chew on. It's what a person would feel when, after a long journey in which he saw everything the world had to offer, he returns to his old, run-down house. I don't belong to the world of packed lunches and the office, but to the one of blood and handcuffs.

•

There isn't much I do well. I excel at only one thing, but it's the kind I can't brag about. Think of the countless people who end up in the grave proud of something they can never share with others.

•

Is there anything more ironic than forgetting to take the meds I need to slow the decline of my cognitive skills? I put dots on the calendar to remind myself to take my pills, but sometimes I forget what the dots mean and stand staring blankly at the calendar.

I remember a bad joke I heard ages ago. A father tells his son to get some candles when the electricity suddenly goes out.

The son says, "Dad, it's so dark. There's no way I'll be able to find the candles."

His father says, "You fool, just turn on the lights and look for them."

My relationship with meds goes something like this joke: I need a decent memory to take the pills, but since that's what I don't have, I can't remember to take them.

•

People want to understand evil. A pointless desire. Evil is like a rainbow. It retreats at the same pace as your approach. Evil is evil because you can't understand it. In medieval Europe, weren't sodomy and homosexuality also sins?

•

Composers probably leave their musical scores behind so that others can play them again in the distant future. When a musical motif comes to a composer, his head must explode in fireworks. In this state, it can't be easy for him to calmly retrieve paper and jot notes down. There's a hint of comedy in the calm of meticulously writing down notations such as *con fuoco*—like fire, with passion. But inside every artist's inner world there is a place for the stifled office clerk. I guess it's necessary. That's how the score, and the composer, will be passed down the generations.

Some composers probably don't leave any written musical scores behind. In the same way, there were likely some powerful martial arts masters who only used their skills to protect themselves and died without passing down their secrets. And the poems I wrote with my victims' blood, my poems that forensics officers call the scene of the crime, are buried in the cabinets of the police station.

•

I keep thinking about future memories, since the future is the very thing I'm trying hard not to forget. I'm fine forgetting the past when I once killed dozens of people. I've lived for decades with no connection to murder. So it's a good thing. But I can't forget the future—namely, my plan. The plan: to kill Pak Jutae. If I forget this future, Eunhui will meet a grisly death at his hands. But my Alzheimer's-diseased brain is doing the opposite: it preserves my oldest memories most vividly, and stubbornly refuses to record the future. It's as if my brain is repeatedly warning me that I don't have a future. But when I think about it, I realize that without a future, the past might have no meaning either.

It's the same for Odysseus. Early on his journey home, Odysseus lands on the island of the Lotus Eaters. After eating the lotus fruit that the locals hospitably urge on him, he forgets about his return home. Not only Odysseus, but all his followers forget as well. The hometown belongs to the past, but plans to return to that home belong to the future. Even afterward, Odysseus continues to struggle with forgetting. He flees the Sirens' song, and escapes from the goddess Calypso, who tries to hold on to him for eternity. The Sirens and Calypso planned to have Odysseus forget the future and remain stuck in the present, but Odysseus resists and aims to return home because he learns that living solely in the present means descending to the life of an animal. You can't call a person who loses all his memories a human being. The present is merely the connecting point for the past and future; it's meaningless alone. What's the difference between a patient with advanced dementia and an animal? Nothing. They eat, shit, laugh and cry, then finally die. Odysseus rejected this. How? By remembering the future, and not giving up on his plans to stride toward the past.

In that sense, my plan to kill Pak is also a kind of homecoming. Maybe my trying to return to the world that I'd left, the era of serial killing, was an attempt to recover who I once was. In this way, my future is connected to my past.

Odysseus had a wife who'd waited anxiously for him. Who

was waiting for me in my dark past? Was it those who died by my hands, those bodies who slept beneath my bamboo forest and babbled on each windswept night? Or was it someone I'd forgotten?

I'm pretty sure the doctor planted something in my head when I had brain surgery. I've heard there's a computer like that. One that, with the press of a button, erases all your records, then self-destructs.

Once again Eunhui doesn't return. It's been how many days already? I can't tell. He hasn't already gotten her, has he? She's not answering her phone, either. It's time to act, but I keep forgetting. I've got to act fast.

I had trouble sleeping, so I went outside and saw the night sky radiant with stars. In the next life I want to return as an astronomer or a lighthouse keeper. Looking back, I realize the hardest part of life is dealing with humans.

I've finished all the prep. Now I just have to get onstage. I do a hundred push-ups. My muscles are tight and firm.

In a dream, I see my naked father going to the bathhouse. I ask, "Father, why are you going to the bathhouse naked?" He answers, "I'll be getting undressed anyway. I might as well go there naked." He had a point. Still, it doesn't feel right, so I ask, "Then why does everyone else go dressed to the bathhouse?" He says, "But you know we're different from the others."

•

I woke up in the morning feeling stiff all over. I ate breakfast and stretched. The stinging in my hands and feet turned out to be light scrapes, so I hunted down the medicine chest to get some ointment. The floors under my feet rustled with sand. Had something happened last night? I didn't remember a thing. There wasn't anything new saved on my recorder when I turned it on. I'd definitely gone somewhere last night, but I must've left it behind. I must have sleepwalked. I wondered if I'd spent the night getting rid of Pak. Yesterday I jotted on my notepad: "I've finished all the prep. Now I just have to get onstage. I do a hundred push-ups. My muscles are tight and firm."

Nothing stood out on TV. The news mentioned nothing about a murder. There was just the weather report. The summer would be unusually hot. The scum—they broadcast the same news every May or June, year after year: "This summer will be unusually hot." It's just a ploy to sell more air conditioners. In early winter, they use another news clip: "This winter will be unusually cold." If all these clips were for real, the earth would be a sauna or a freezer by now.

I watch the news all day. They must not have discovered Pak's corpse yet. It'd be dangerous for me to hang around in the area, so I stay put. Does the corpse even exist? The dried dirt up my arm makes me think I've buried him somewhere, but I'm frustrated because I can't remember. How will Eunhui react if she discovers his corpse? What will she do afterward?

Will she learn years later what a difficult act I'd committed for her sake? What about the police? Will they discover that Pak was the serial killer who had driven the neighborhood into a cauldron of fear? Maybe that's too much to hope for.

I took a shower. I washed thoroughly, then burned the clothes I'd been wearing. I vacuumed the entire house and burned whatever was in the dust bag. Then I poured bleach into the bag, finally washed and dried it. Then I asked myself, Why bother? I'd forget it all anyway. If caught, wouldn't I finally end up in the jail cell that I'd only seen in my fantasies? What was so bad about departing the confusing world of dust for a world of iron divided into rigid square frames?

•

Today I listened all day long to Beethoven's Piano Concerto No. 5 ("Emperor").

•

I read this in the papers a while ago: A terminally ill cancer patient asked the hospital staff to call the police. He then confessed to a murder he'd committed ten years before. He had kidnapped his business partner and killed him. The police discovered the partner's remains buried on a small mountain. Returning to the hospital, they found the murderer in a coma and near death. He'd had to bear the guilt on top of the intense physical pain, so the public forgave him. Everyone must have assumed that he was paying for his sins. But would I also be forgiven? What would they say to a serial killer who had slipped painlessly into oblivion and even forgotten who he was?

•

I'm completely alert today. Do I really have dementia?

•

Why isn't Eunhui back? She isn't answering her cell phone, either. Has she found out who I really am? No, not possible.

•

I took a walk in the bamboo forest. The bamboo sprouts were growing rapidly upward. Something connected to the green shoots began coming back to me, then disappeared. I looked at the sky. The bamboo leaves rustled in the wind. I felt calmer, at peace. I didn't know whose bamboo forest it was, but I liked it. I wandered through the entire village. There was something I needed to find, but what it was, I couldn't remember.

I opened my journal and read something I'd written about Pak Jutae and his jeep, about how often the bastard kept showing up and monitoring me. I walked through the village one more time. There was no sign of Pak or his jeep. No doubt he died at my hands. I feel proud that I defeated the young bastard, but it also feels futile, since I recall absolutely nothing. I'm not one to collect trophies—I'd trusted my memory to meticulously record what happened. Frankly, if I can't remember, what use is a victim's ring or barrette? I wouldn't even know where it came from.

•

I sat on the back veranda and watched twilight fall over the village. Is this how life ends?

•

Stray dogs are known to dig tunnels under front gates and crawl onto people's property. Once they end up on the streets, even house pets instantly act like wolves. They howl at the moon, dig holes, and adapt to the new social codes. Even pregnancy has a hierarchy: only the head female can have babies. If a low-ranking female somehow ends up pregnant, the others attack and kill her. A yellow mutt who's dug in my yard for a few days is walking around with an object in his mouth. This mutt from nowhere. What did he bring me this time? I threatened him with a stick until he cowered and fled. I used the stick to turn over the pale object covered with dirt.

A girl's hand.

•

Either Pak Jutae is still alive or I had the wrong man. It's one or the other.

•

Eunhui's still not answering her phone.

•

An Alzheimer's patient is like a traveler who mixes up his dates and arrives a day early at the airport. Until he reaches the ticket counter, he's as sure of himself as a rock. He calmly hands his passport and ticket over the counter. The attendant shakes her head and says, "I'm sorry, but you've come a day early," but he believes the attendant is wrong.

He says, "Please check your system one more time."

Another staff member joins and says that the customer has mixed up the dates. Only then does the man admit he is wrong and retreat. The next day, when he comes to the counter and shows his ticket, another attendant tells him the same thing: "You've come a day early."

This scene repeats itself daily. He ends up eternally wandering around the airport, unable to arrive on time. He isn't trapped in the present, but flounders in a space that isn't past, present, or future. No one understands him. As his loneliness and fear escalate, he becomes a man who does nothing. No, he's changing into a man who can't do anything.

•

I was sitting dumbly in my car, parked at the curb. I didn't know why I was there. A patrol car stopped behind me, then a young cop knocked on my window. I didn't recognize him.

He asked, "Sir, what are you doing here?"

"I'm not sure myself."

"Sir, where do you live?"

I dug out my vehicle registration papers one by one and showed him.

"Could you please give me your driver's license, too?"

I did what he told me to. The policeman looked straight at me and asked, "What brings you out here at this time of night?"

"I told you, I don't know."

"Please follow me. You do know how to drive, correct?"

I turned on the hazard lights and followed his car into the village. Only when I was home did I remember: I had been heading to Pak's house to find Eunhui. I was thirsty, so I opened the fridge. I saw a hand in a plastic bag.

Could that really be Eunhui's hand? God, for some reason I can't stop thinking that it's her hand. Otherwise, why was it sent to me? Since Pak is alive, he's boldly sent me the hand. The bastard is challenging me to a game, but I can't even make it to his house. No, even if I broke into his house, I would never defeat him. My entire body trembles with rage, knowing I have no choice but to take his taunts.

I turned the room inside out looking for Detective Ahn's business card so I could call him. With nothing to lose, nothing scared me. But no matter how much I looked, I couldn't find his card. I was forced to call 112 and say, "My daughter's been murdered, and I think I know who her killer is. Please come quickly, before I forget."

•

Oedipus was on the road when, in a fit of anger, he killed someone. Then he forgot about it. The first time I read this, I was impressed that he could forget such a thing.

When an epidemic rages across Thebes, King Oedipus orders the criminal who has offended the gods to be captured. But before the day's end, he learns that he is that very criminal. In this moment, does he feel shame or guilt? It's probably shame for sleeping with his mother, and guilt for killing his father.

If Oedipus looks into the mirror, he'll see me standing there. We look the same, but the image is flipped. Though we are both murderers, he doesn't realize that the person he killed was his father and even forgets that he killed a man. Only later does he come to know what he has done, and gouges out his eyes.

From the start, I was aware that I was killing my father, had known that I would kill him. Afterward, I never forgot. The rest of the murders were a mere chorus to the first one. Each time my hands were covered in blood, I sensed the shadow of the first murder. But in the last act of my life, I'll forget about all the evil I've committed. As a result, I'll become someone who doesn't need to—someone unable to—forgive himself. Though a blind Oedipus becomes enlightened and wise in old age, I become a child. I'll be a ghostly figure who can't be held responsible.

Oedipus proceeded from ignorance to forgetting, and from forgetting to destruction. I'm the exact opposite. I'll transition from destruction to forgetting, then from forgetting to ignorance, pure ignorance.

·

Plainclothes detectives knocked on the front door. I got dressed and opened the door for them. Behind the detectives were uniformed cops.

I asked, "Are you coming because of the 112 call?"

"Yes. Are you Kim Byeongsu?"

"Yes, that's correct."

I handed over the plastic bag.

One man asked, "So the dog came with this in his mouth?"

"That's right."

"Can we search the premises?"

"There's no need to search here. You have to get the criminal."

"Who is it? Do you know?"

"It's the bastard Pak Jutae. He's in real estate and goes hunting in the area . . ."

The detectives laughed and smirked. A man standing behind the police abruptly emerged up front.

He said, "Are you talking about me?"

It was Pak. He was with them. My legs went weak, my eyes

83

searched them. Were they in it together? I pointed at Pak and shouted, "Get the bastard!"

Pak laughed. Something warm trickled down my thigh. What was this?

"The old man's pissed his pants." They couldn't stop laughing and snickering.

Shaking, I collapsed onto the veranda. German shepherds came in through the gaping front gate.

A middle-aged detective in a leather jacket said, "Give him the warrant, though who knows if he'll recognize it."

As soon as the order was given, a younger cop shoved a piece of paper at me.

"Here, you've seen the warrant. We'll start the search now."

After one of the shepherds sniffed around a corner of the yard, he barked sharply three times. One of the uniformed police began digging with a shovel.

"Ah, here it is."

"But something's not right."

With one look you could tell that it was a child's remains. A bony white skeleton, it had clearly been buried for years. The police start a discussion among themselves. The locals are just outside, crowding against the gate. The cops put up a police line. The police seem either disturbed or excited, I'm not sure which. I've always been slow at reading people's expressions. And who was that kid? They're saying she was buried long ago, but why can't I remember anything? Why is Pak with the police?

•

I'm behind bars. The police keep coming for me. They keep talking about "yesterday," but I have no recall of "yesterday."

Each interrogation feels like the first one, so I always start from the beginning. I tell them how many people I've killed and that I never got caught; about the kinds of poems I wrote; about why I didn't kill the poetry instructor; about Nietzsche, Homer, and Sophocles, how the three keenly understood the life and death of man.

The police don't want to hear any of this. They don't seem interested in my proud past or my philosophy. They believe I killed Eunhui, and they focus only on that. I tell them Pak Jutae probably killed her. I say that he had been seeing Eunhui. I say that since I collided with his car and saw blood dripping from his trunk, he's been keeping an eye on me.

The detective in front of me smirks, laughs, then says, "When he's a cop?"

I protest. Isn't a cop also capable of murder?

He nods readily. "Of course that's possible. But probably not this time."

I look for Detective Ahn. He of all people might believe me. Again, the detective ruthlessly shakes his head. He says he doesn't know a Detective Ahn. I describe his appearance in great detail, his way of speaking, and what we talked about. One of the police detectives says, "For someone who says he has no short-term memory, how can you remember this Detective Ahn so clearly?"

The man's right, but why am I so angry?

•

I feel like I've ended up in a parallel universe. Here, Pak Jutae is a cop, Detective Ahn doesn't exist, and I've become Eunhui's murderer.

•

85

The police detectives come for me again. Again one asks me, "Why did you kill Kim Eunhui?"

"Pak Jutae killed my daughter."

As if I wasn't there, the middle-aged detective leans toward the younger one and says, "What's the use of questioning him?"

"Still, we have to write up a report. It could be an act for all we know."

The younger detective says he's had enough, and says to me, "Look here, Kim. Eunhui is not your daughter. She's your caregiver, someone who assists the elderly with dementia."

I don't know what a caregiver is. The middle-aged one holds back the increasingly angry younger one, saying, "Your blood pressure'll go up. Forget it. Nothing you say will make a difference."

•

Confusion is watching over me.

•

I discovered my story in the paper. I tore it out and kept it.

The family of Kim Eunhui reported her absence to the police when Kim, who rarely missed work, was unreachable by phone and had missed work for four days. The police investigating Kim's whereabouts focused on her work as a caregiver for dementia patients. They followed up on her patients, and after determining that Kim Byeongsu, aged 70, was a prime suspect, issued a warrant. On searching his property, they discovered Kim Eunhui's corpse as well as dismembered parts of her body. Not only was Kim's corpse found, but a child's skeleton was also uncovered. Based on the skeleton's condition, the police hypothesize that the child was secretly buried years earlier. Investigation of the child's murder will continue once the identification results from the National Forensic Service are confirmed. The suspect Kim Byeongsu has no previous criminal record, and is known to have advanced Alzheimer's disease. Interest is rising in whether the prosecution and indictment will continue.

•

I keep appearing on television. No one believes that Eunhui is my daughter. Since everyone is saying that, I wonder if I'm wrong after all. They say that Eunhui was a responsible caregiver who selflessly aided dementia patients without families. A scene of her colleagues crying during her funeral repeatedly flashes on the screen. They are sobbing so sorrowfully that even I almost believe that she wasn't my daughter but an actual professional caregiver. The police are uprooting the area around my house. They mention words like "genetic testing" and "demon."

I called the detective and told him to stop digging in the yard and start instead in the bamboo forest. The detective went outside, looking tense. From that point, the bamboo forest appeared on TV. My bamboo forest, whose brilliant leaves always sang melodies to me.

As waterproof bags filled with skeletons descended the mountain one by one, one of the locals reported, "What it is, is a—a cemetery, a cemetery."

•

Incomprehensible things continue without end. Similar events in similar situations continue to repeat themselves, and I'm completely lost. I can't remember anything anymore. Here I don't have a pen or recorder. I think they took them away. I just manage to get a piece of chalk and record each day on the wall. Sometimes I wonder why I bother. Everything is so mixed up.

•

I was dragged to an inspection of the crime scene, but I didn't do anything. Meaning, I couldn't do anything. How can I re-enact a scene I can't remember? One of the locals threw a bottle at me, saying I was no better than an animal. The bottle hit me in the forehead. It hurt.

•

Pak came for me. I'm so confused every time I see him. He said it was true that he had tailed me for some time. He said he'd suspected that I might be connected to the multiple murders in the district. As soon as he sat down, a psychologist followed and sat beside him. He resembled the man on TV who talked about the psychology of a serial killer, but maybe not.

Pak asked, "Do you remember my visit with the students from the Police Academy?"

"That was Detective Ahn."

"There is no Detective Ahn. I was the one who brought the students."

I strongly denied this. Pak looked at the psychologist. I didn't miss them exchanging smiles.

"That's not true," I said. "You came with Eunhui. You said you were going to marry her."

"I did meet Kim Eunhui. Since she was at your house regularly, I also had a few questions for her."

"But didn't I hit your car? Your jeep. How can you explain that?"

"That couldn't have happened. I drive a Hyundai."

"You're saying you don't hunt, either?"

"No."

The more we talked, the more confused I got. Last, I asked, "Did the killings stop?"

"It's too early to tell. We'll have to wait and see."

The psychologist and Pak exchanged meaningful smiles, then exited the room, leaving me alone.

•

Some days I'm alert, and others, I feel dazed.

•

The detective asks me, "Do you feel wronged?"

I shake my head.

"Do you believe you've been falsely accused?"

That made me laugh. The detective is underestimating me. That offends me the most. If they'd caught me in time, the sentence would have been much worse. If it was during Park Chung-hee's regime, they would have immediately hanged me or sent me to the electric chair.

I killed Eunhui's mother. After first killing Eunhui's father at their house, I kidnapped her mother while she was leaving work and killed her. Eunhui was at daycare, so she escaped. I still remember each of those scenes vividly. But I don't remember anything about Eunhui's own death, though the police seem to have found the tools that I used to kill and bury her. I must have left some things out in the back. My fingerprints were apparently found all over the tools. When the cops decide to get you, there's nothing they won't do.

I once heard about an artist who had made so many paintings that he couldn't tell if one of them was forged or not. While claiming it was a fake, he said, "It looks like one of my paintings, but I don't remember painting it."

The painter finally lost the suit. I knew exactly how he felt.

I said to the detective, "It seems like something I'd do, but I've no memory of it."

He urged me to remember, adding, "How can you kill someone and not remember?"

I grabbed his hand. He didn't push me away. I looked into his eyes and said, "You don't understand. I want to remember what happened more than anyone. Mister, I do want to remember, because it's so precious to me."

•

People say my memories of Eunhui are false. No one's on my side. I even heard a person say on TV, "After retiring as a veterinarian, he had little contact with his neighbors and lived the secluded life of a loner. I never once saw family visit him."

One day I asked the detective, "Then did I have a dog? The yellow mutt?"

"The dog? Oh, that dog. Yes, there was a dog. The one that dug up your lawn."

I felt a little reassured knowing that the yellow mutt did exist.

"What happened to the dog? After what happened to his owners . . ."

"What do you mean, 'his owners'? There's only you." He called out, "Hey, what happened to the dog? The mutt?"

The young detective, carrying some papers for him, said, "The locals wanted to eat it, since it's got no owner. But the village head said, 'What would they become if they ate a dog that had devoured human flesh?' So they let it go. Since he's got no one caring for him, I guess he'll end up a stray."

•

I heard something about Eunhui on TV: "Colleagues are devastated by the death of Kim Eunhui, a woman who selflessly devoted herself to helping those with dementia."

What about all my conversations with her? Had I made them all up? That's impossible. How could the imagination be more real than what I'm experiencing right now?

•

I asked, "Did you find a lot of skeletons?"

The detective nodded.

I said, "Let me ask you one thing. Way back, I killed a woman who worked at the downtown community center and her husband. Could you find out if they had a child?"

He said he would. The cops aren't hostile to me anymore. Sometimes they seem to have respect for me. They even seem to consider me some sort of courageous whistle-blower.

A few days later, the detective returned and said, "They had a three-year-old baby, but she was killed along with her father. With a blunt weapon."

The cop went through his documents and grinned. "Funny coincidence. The dead kid's name was Eunhui, too."

•

I suddenly realize I've lost. I don't know at what. I just feel as if I've lost.

•

Time passes. The trial begins. People swarm in. I'm moved from here to there. People rush in again. I'm moved here and there. They crowd in again. People begin asking me about my past. I'm able to respond relatively well to these questions. I talk about the acts I committed in the past without stopping, and people write it all down. I tell them everything except about killing my father. They ask me, "How can you remember things so clearly from long ago but can't remember crimes you'd recently committed? That makes no sense." And wasn't I being open about the past because the statute of limitations had passed, but not confessing to recent crimes because I was afraid of being sentenced?

People don't understand that I'm being punished this very minute. God has already decided how to punish me. I am stepping into forgetting.

•

Will I become a zombie when I die? Or was I already one?

•

A man who said he was a journalist visited me. He said he wanted to understand evil.

What he said was so clichéd, it amused me.

I said, "Why are you trying to understand evil?"

"I'd have to understand it in order to avoid it."

I said, "If you can understand it, then it isn't evil. Just stick to praying, so you can stay out of evil's way."

His disappointment was obvious.

I added, "Evil isn't what's terrifying. It's time. No one can defeat time."

•

I'm somewhere that could be a jail or a hospital. I can't distinguish between the two anymore. Maybe I'm drifting between the two. It feels like a day or two has passed, or an eternity. It's impossible to tell. I can't tell if it's morning or afternoon. Or if it's this life or that life. Strangers visit and keep asking me about different people. None of those names stir up any images in me anymore. Whatever links the names of objects, people, and feelings has been destroyed. I am isolated on a tiny spot in the vast universe, and I'll never escape it.

•

Over the past few days, a poem has been circling in my head like a swarm of mayflies by a riverbank. It was written by a Japanese death row inmate.

> *The rest of*
> *the song*
> *I shall hear in the afterlife,*
> *over here.*

A complete stranger sits in front of me and begins talking. He looks tough and scares me a little.

He questions me closely, saying, "Are you just pretending to have dementia? To avoid being sentenced?"

I say, "I don't have dementia. I'm just forgetful, that's all."

"Didn't you first claim you had dementia?"

"Me? I don't remember saying that. I don't have dementia. I'm just a little tired. No, not a little—I'm exhausted."

While he shakes his head from side to side, he jots something down on paper. He asks, "Why did you kill Kim Eunhui? What was your motive?"

"Me? When? Who?"

He keeps talking about things I can't understand, and I become unbearably tired. I hang my head and begin begging. I say, "If I've done something wrong, please forgive me."

•

It's hard to wake up. I have no idea what time it is, or whether it's morning or night.

•

I can barely understand what people are saying.

•

Only now do I truly understand a passage from the Heart Sutra that I must have memorized. I sit on the bed and repeatedly chant it to myself:

> *So, in the emptiness, no form,*
> *No feeling, thought, or choice,*
> *Nor is there consciousness.*
> *No eyes, ears, nose, tongue, body, mind.*
> *No color, sound, smell, taste, touch,*
> *Or what the mind takes hold of,*
> *Nor even act of sensing.*
> *No ignorance or end of it,*
> *Nor all that comes of ignorance.*

No withering, no death,
No end of them.
Nor is there pain, or cause of pain,
Or cease in pain, or noble path
To lead from pain.
Not even wisdom to attain!
Attainment, too, is emptiness.

•

I'm floating in lukewarm water. It's peaceful, tranquil. Who am I? And where is this place? A gentle breeze blows into the emptiness. I continue swimming, but no matter how much I paddle my arms, I can't escape. This silent, still world becomes smaller and smaller. It becomes infinitely small until it becomes a single dot. It becomes a speck of dust in the cosmos. No, even that disappears.

THE ORIGIN OF LIFE

Each time Seojin encountered difficulty in his life, he longed to return to his origins. Back to the place he'd left, what people usually called "the hometown." Back to where everyone knew who he was. But no matter how much he thought about it, he wasn't sure where that was. He had lived a drifter's life. When he was young he had moved repeatedly across the country with his parents, and when he was older he hadn't managed to stay in one place. It was the same with people; he had no relationships that had deepened with time. Long ago, he'd watched a film in which the main character shouted, "I want to go back!" But Seojin had felt jealous of him, not sympathetic. To have somewhere to return to resembled a valuable achievement that would never be his. Such achievements came easily to some. That someone like him could never possess it, no matter how hard they tried, felt truly unfair.

"We should never have met," said Ina. Ina had the ability

to talk about happiness as if she was speaking about regret. She looked as if she couldn't believe in such undeserved happiness, which perplexed Seojin. She would gaze out at magnificent scenery and say, "We shouldn't have come here." And when he asked why, she was the type who would respond, "Because it makes the past feel that much more terrible." For someone as severely anxious about human bonds as Seojin, the discord between her regretful tone and her happy expression was much sweeter. Sometimes just to savor that sweetness, he would ask her, "Do you regret meeting me?" even as he anticipated her response.

Ina traced the rim of her beer glass with her index finger and said, "I do. If I hadn't met you, I wouldn't have realized how beautiful life was, and I would have thought that living like everyone else is the only way to live. I would've endured, and after enduring, I would have simply died. Then I would've had little to regret."

Seojin took Ina's hand. "I don't regret it," he said. "Everything that happened before I met you reminds me of a recent dream. You know how no matter what you dream about, in the morning you always wake up in the same place you were the night before."

"I wish I could see it the way you do."

"You're where I begin."

"What does that mean?" she asked.

"It's not important. But it's what I've always looked for."

They had been classmates in the fifth grade. They both transferred to the same school on the same day. They had gotten on the school bus for military kids, and greeted each other in typical military family fashion.

"My dad's deputy chief of staff for logistics."

"My dad's deputy chief of staff for operations."

Their fathers also had similar ranks, both lieutenant colonels.

The bus passed rice paddies and farmland, then let the kids off at the military's family housing. When Ina casually said "See you tomorrow" before she headed into her house, Seojin felt his heart flutter for the first time. It felt as if a whisk was stirring up his heart.

At school they said little to each other, since the girls stuck with the girls and the boys stuck with the boys. But once they returned to the family housing, they had a lot of free time. There were no after-school cram schools around, and the television reception was poor, so in that remote area near the North-South border they often met and talked about the few books they'd read. They both owned a complete set of biographies of famous people, put out by the same publisher, and since in their small world the few grown-ups they encountered were their parents and teachers, they naturally began to adopt primarily Western characters into their games of make-believe. Unlike Seojin, who was attracted to playing the part of conquest-driven, rural-born characters such as Napoleon, Ina preferred playing characters renowned in science and medicine, such as Marie Curie and Florence Nightingale.

Ina said, "Napoleon killed too many people."

Seojin didn't give in to Ina's tactics, and said, "If Curie hadn't been born, the atomic bomb wouldn't exist."

"If a man kills a lot of people, I guess he's revered as a great person."

"I like Mozart, too. He was a genius."

"I think Beethoven's more amazing. I mean, he lost his hearing but overcame it."

It was a childish conversation, but Seojin enjoyed every minute of it. He imagined the distant future in which he became famous, and reveled in the thought that if that happened, Ina would be proud of him. But Seojin kept all this to himself. Spring quickly turned into summer, and summer into fall. In the fall, rumors began to float within the housing compound about promotions and transfers. Out of all the deputy chiefs of staff for operations, Ina's father was first to be promoted to colonel and was simultaneously appointed to the army's headquarters. Seojin's father was passed over for promotion and was transferred to the border. The day Ina's family moved, Seojin presented her with a farewell gift, a model Spanish galleon that had taken him over a month to build. It had been challenging to glue together each single pin set of the countless pieces of the Age of Exploration–style galleon. On closer look, there were adorable oars and cannons, even a model sailor atop the mainmast, gazing through a spyglass.

"Remember that boat you gave me?" said Ina. "I still have it."

Twenty years later, they had unexpectedly run into each other by a lake near a new town's apartment complex.

Seojin had gone for a run, and Ina had been sitting on a bench reading a magazine. Ina, pleased to see him, brought up the Spanish galleon. She said, "My husband once asked me about the boat."

"So what did you say?"

"I said I got it as a present when I was young, but that was all I remembered."

"Your parents are doing well?"

"My father retired as lieutenant general, but he passed away suddenly in his sleep. Officially it was a heart attack, but it was actually suicide. It must've been a huge shock to my mother—she died not many years after."

Seojin owned a small medical devices supplier, and as for Ina, she had stopped working as a contract English teacher in a middle school. Her husband was in finance, and they had decided not to have children. In broad daylight, while at a motel, Seojin discovered bruises across Ina's body. Her husband. She had stopped teaching because as the number of beatings increased, so had her absences from school. The bruises seemed to be talking directly to Seojin: You may think this woman is yours, but the real owner is elsewhere. I can beat her, take her job away from her, even destroy her if I want, because it's me who's her legally wedded husband.

Every time Seojin saw evidence of new beatings, he became furious at Ina's husband and said things like, "The crazy son of a bitch, I'm going to kill him." And each time, Ina said, "I knew we shouldn't have ever met. Then things would've stayed the same . . ."

She spoke as if Seojin himself were responsible for the beatings and the resulting shame. That it sounded as if she regretted meeting him—not her marriage, but meeting him— made him even more furious. He'd asked her repeatedly to get a divorce and start a new life with him instead, but Ina would wave her hand dismissively and say, "You think divorce is child's play?"

She said, "I often thought I'd end up dead if things kept on this way. Once he turned the gas range on and tried to shove my head over it. And one day he kicked me in the stomach and I flew three feet in the air. Sometimes I wish it were all over."

Frustrated, Seojin would offer all kinds of advice, from getting a medical report, to reporting her husband to the police, to going for counseling. But Ina only looked repulsed and dismissed his advice.

She said, "Just stop it. These moments together are the only times I breathe freely, so why are you making the problem worse? Even if it's only for a short while, being with you makes me happy. Can't we just stay the way we are?"

"How can I do nothing when the person I love is being pummeled every day?"

Ina looked squarely in his eyes. "There's a big difference between what you think you can do and what you can actually do. Most people are like that. Right now, you probably feel that you would do anything for me. Of course, I know you really mean it. But no hard and fast rule says you'll act just because you really mean it."

Seojin sensed then that Ina had already repeatedly experienced such moments in the past, that she had lived through this scene they were playing out, and that it was merely one of many such moments in her future. Why would Ina, in such a troubled marriage, have opened up to him alone? Men before Seojin had made promises to her, then fled and abandoned her at crucial moments. Though Ina was the origin that Seojin returned to, wasn't Seojin a shelter for her during the arduous trek of her life? Unlike the origin that she was for him, one might be tearfully grateful at the sight of a shelter, but there was always yet another shelter. Seojin fervently desired to be the one-and-only for Ina. But he wasn't sure how to become that person.

Seojin began each day with an early-morning run in the park surrounding the lake. The young saplings gave little shade, but the place was ideal for running. One lap around the lake equaled two and a half miles, and Seojin always did a fast two laps around it. One day he was nimbly doing a lap when a man sprang out abruptly from behind a group of spindle trees, and unable to dodge him, Seojin stumbled to the ground. When the man approached, Seojin assumed that he would offer him a hand and apologize. Instead, the man merely looked down at Seojin and gave him a nasty smile.

After watching Seojin pick himself up, the man said, "Does this situation require an apology from me?"

Seojin hadn't expected such a response, and he wondered if he'd made the mistake. He found himself saying, "It's fine, there's no need."

"Well, then."

Without a word of apology, the man, wearing a tracksuit with a large Adidas logo emblazoned on the back, ran off in the opposite direction. After man disappeared, Seojin stayed put and mulled over what had just happened. Adidas hadn't made the slightest attempt to slow down and had charged like a quarterback running with a football. If the stranger hadn't collided with Seojin, inertia would have sent him running straight into the lake. No matter how he considered it, the only possibility was that the man had deliberately attacked him. He checked himself over in case he had been mugged, but he'd carried nothing with him.

"Does this situation require an apology from me?" That the perpetrator could coolly say this to his confused victim made Seojin feel increasingly annoyed and leery. The tumble had left his body creaking, and he felt sore from his neck down to his waist.

From that day on, he began running into the man everywhere he went. He'd be at the bank and glimpse the man seated on a sofa, or on the way to work find himself in line in front of or behind the man at his regular coffee shop. Of course he wore a suit and not workout clothes. The man didn't avoid his gaze, and each time their eyes met he would give Seojin the same nasty smile that sent the phrase "Does this situation require an apology from me?" echoing in Seojin's head. One day he realized that the man might be Ina's husband.

Once he was entertaining hospital officials at a hostess bar when the man entered the private room and said, "This isn't our room?"

He glanced quickly at Seojin, then left. Seojin was drunk enough by then to jump up and follow him out. The man, who was going up the steps to the first floor, looked back at him.

The man said, "What is it?" and stood in his way.

Seojin felt a little afraid; one kick from the man would be enough to send him tumbling down. He tried moving up to the man's level, but the stranger blocked his way as if taunting him.

"I said, what is it?" The man pressed him again.

Seojin had no choice but to confront him. He said, "Why are you following me? Who the hell are you?"

"Let's say I'm here about an emotional debt."

"You're saying you owe me?"

"No, you owe *me*. You owe me hugely."

"I've got no idea what you're talking about."

He spat out through gritted teeth, "You're fooling around with another man's girl and you still don't get it?"

Seojin recalled the man's words from the first run-in, and

now he had an unbearable urge to repeat "Does this situation require an apology from me?" But he had more self-restraint than most, and instead said, "I think you've got the wrong person."

"I guess she never told you about my line of work. You can't do my kind of work and pick the wrong person."

He pointed two fingers at his own eyes. It was as if his fingers were a well-sharpened knife.

"I've got to be real good at getting the right person to make any progress at all. It's the same when I loan money to people, and when I go after the shits who run without paying their debts."

So the husband who she'd said worked in finance was actually a loan shark. Seojin had never borrowed money from one of them, but knew of their notorious rep. He noted the man's small but firm fists. From the lower step where he was standing, he was at eye level with those fists. A tattoo on one of the man's wrists went up his forearm.

Seojin only repeated, "You've got the wrong person," as he slowly descended backwards down the steps and returned to his group. The man didn't pursue him.

Sleep didn't come easily that night for Seojin. It felt as if the man would burst into his life anytime and destroy it. When he considered the high compound interest increasing daily on his emotional debt, the hair on the back of his neck stood up. How do you repay an emotional debt? Was there a cash equivalent for it? He had no idea.

From that day on, Seojin avoided Ina's calls. He said he was busy and barely texted back when she messaged him; he'd begun to suspect that Adidas was using high-tech surveillance gear to intercept his calls and texts. It might be difficult to pay back his loan, but he didn't want to fall further into debt. His fear of Ina's husband outweighed his longing to see her. Adidas would know that Seojin had reflected on his behavior and avoided meeting her, and he might even forgive him. At first Ina was bewildered by Seojin's change of heart, but she seemed to slowly accept their breakup. Although Ina was resigned, she didn't bother to hide her disappointment when he abruptly got off the phone. He felt guilty in those moments. Sometimes Ina sent him late-night texts hinting at her husband's terrible violence:

"Another nightmarish night. But I'll have to overcome it. It makes me so sad to think there's no one I can turn to, but what can I do? I chose this life. I won't burden you. You don't have to respond to this, just don't erase my message. I feel stronger just knowing I can tell someone the truth."

He began habitually scoping out his surroundings wherever he went. He even quit jogging at dawn, since he'd start gasping for breath at the thought that at any minute Adidas could hurtle into him. Thankfully, nothing had happened yet. Adidas seemed to know that he was no longer meeting Ina.

Eventually Ina's infrequent phone calls stopped altogether. He began to worry. Was she beaten so badly that she'd ended up in a hospital somewhere, or had something even worse happened? He was so anxious that his lips became parched and chapped, but he didn't want to contact her first. For all he knew, Ina might have finally gotten over him. She would recover; she was a strong kid, he repeated to himself each night while drinking whiskey or brandy before bed.

One day Ina contacted him out of the blue at around three in the morning. The text, unlike her typical messages, was terse: "Can you come over?"

He felt apprehensive, but as usual he didn't reply. Instead, he waited and had another two shots of whiskey, straight. His phone stayed silent as if he'd never received the text. Did the alcohol erode his usual self-control? He couldn't wait any longer and called her, and when she answered, she repeated listlessly, "Can you come over?"

He asked, "What's the matter?"

"I'm sorry. I had no one else to turn to. Help me — it's the last thing I'll ever ask you for. I won't bother you anymore after this."

"Where are you?"

She told him her address.

"Isn't that your home address?"

"Yeah, I'm at home."

"Your husband?"

"It's okay. Just come over. I need help, fast." She repeated, "It's the last thing I'll ever ask of you."

Seojin took his car and raced over to Ina's apartment. Before he had a chance to ring the bell, the front door opened.

Ina's hair was knotty and her face puffy as if she had been beaten up. She said, "You really came."

The house was a mess. He saw bloodstains on the floor and guessed what had happened: he had walked into the kind of crime scene he'd seen only on the news. An abused wife had lost control and killed her husband, then gotten her lover involved.

He said, "Where's your husband?"

She pointed toward the bedroom. Just inside he spotted the dusty galleon in a display cabinet, and he was a little startled by its puny size. He'd believed that he constructed an enormous, stately sailing ship, but it was merely a cheap kid's toy. As soon as he entered the bedroom, his foot caught on a golf club. A four iron. He saw a man sprawled facedown at the bathroom door. As if her husband had been hit with the club, the crown of his head was caked in blood.

Her voice trembling, Ina asked, "What should I do? Is this how my life ends?"

Seojin looked bewildered and said, "What were you thinking, calling me after making this mess?"

Ina faltered back, as if she had just discovered her husband's murderer. Seojin grabbed her by the arm. "Where are you going?"

Ina protested, asking, "Does this situation require an apology from me?"

He let go of her arm.

She said, "You work in the medical industry, so you know a lot of doctors, don't you? So I just wanted to ask you. Can't you give me an answer? You can't do that much for me?"

Seojin was astounded. Just as her husband the loan shark was in the finance industry, was a medical supply salesman part of the medical industry? Even if he were an actual doctor, what could he do in these circumstances?

"Call 112. There's no way out. Call and say that your husband was beating you, and you killed him in self-defense. What choice do you have? They'll consider your circumstances. I told you before to keep the medical reports. If you submit those, you'll be fine."

"Oh. Thanks for the advice," she said. "You're more pragmatic than I thought."

She collapsed onto the sofa, muttering, "I'm scared, so scared."

"You actually expected me to do something about the corpse? Make it disappear, like magic?"

"Don't get angry. I was just so scared."

As she burst into tears, Seojin sat down and held her. She began telling him why she'd had no choice but to defend herself. Only then Seojin began regretting his cool logical behavior. He still had feelings for her, and she had suffered so much. He was also a little proud that at the most crucial moment of her life, she had called him. He was with her at what would probably be her life's single most critical juncture.

He held her trembling body and made a rash promise: "At most you'll get two or three years. It could be even shorter if they accept the self-defense plea. Once you're out, let's get married. I'll wait for you."

She looked up tearfully at him. "Do you mean it?"

"Of course. Forget the past. Consider it a long nightmare. After the trial I'll visit you weekly while you're in jail, make wedding preparations, get the house ready . . ."

Her voice dropped as she said, "We should never have met."

"What do you mean?"

"We've both ended up unhappy. I'll go to jail, and you'll be stuck in the middle of all this, then end up being responsible for me."

A thud came from the bedroom, as if a hefty object had bumped into the door. Seojin and Ina stared at each other. Terrified, Ina buried her head in her knees, while Seojin cautiously approached the bedroom and pushed the door ajar. A man covered in blood was crawling out. Ina moaned. The man was using the doorknob to raise himself up when his eyes met Seojin's. More shocking to Seojin than the dead man come to life was this: the man wasn't the loan shark.

"Oh my God. Oh my God." Ina's entire body trembled.

The man just managed to stand. He stared suspiciously at Seojin. As Seojin slowly stepped back, the man tried to grab him but fell when his knees gave out. Seojin caught him in his arms and broke his fall. He laid him on the floor. The man had fainted again but his breathing was regular.

"Who is this man?"

"He's my husband. Who else would he be?"

Her eyes met Seojin's. Her eyes were cold and frigid, as if she blamed Seojin for reviving her husband.

"He is?"

"What do you mean?"

"Nothing."

Ina continued gazing worriedly at her husband.

"Call 119 now," Seojin pressed her.

"You just keep telling me to call someone, first the police, now an ambulance." She sobbed and buried her head in her lap.

"What do I do now? I mean, how do I go on? Have I no choice but to help him recover and then keep living with him?"

There was nothing he could say to her. Even if he had something to say, he didn't want to say it.

"There's no reason you would understand," she said. "Life —we have to keep going even if sometimes we don't have answers. It isn't your life anyway. Once you leave, it's over for you."

She looked resigned as she finally called 119 on her cell phone. She calmly fabricated a story about how her husband, drunk, had slipped in the bathroom and hurt his head. She said that he had come to for a moment, then fainted again.

"Yes, his breathing is stable . . . Yes, he's breathing. He's unconscious."

She hung up and said, "You can go now. It'll look bad if you're here."

He was putting his shoes on when he turned back to Ina. "Oh, back there you said, 'Does this situation require an apology from me?'"

"I did?"

"Yeah, I definitely heard you. Where did you first hear that?"

"Does that matter right now? I don't remember. It's a pretty normal thing to say."

"You don't think it's unusual? It's—"

"Stop it, please. Just go."

"Look, something strange has been going on with me—"

"I said leave. I think I hear an ambulance."

He took the elevator down to the underground parking lot. He sat in the car and thought. Something was truly off. *Who was the man who hurtled into me at the lake, going on about an emotional debt?* He decided he had to find the man. As he drove home, the rays of streetlights ahead went filmy behind him. The lights resembled the life that had nearly been his. He drove past his life wedded to Ina after she finished her prison sentence, his life spent terrorized at the mere sight of the police after helping Ina get rid of the corpse, his life as a criminal after murdering Ina's half-conscious husband. He imagined headlines such as "Unfaithful Housewife," "Affair Behind Conspiracy," "Husband Murdered, Then Reported Missing." Only now, after he left those possibilities behind, he imagined Ina's future. What would her husband do to a wife who had nearly killed him? On top of that, he'd run directly into his wife's lover. She could end up dying at her husband's hands. Seojin couldn't block out the thought, but it was too late to go back.

Ten days later, Ina jumped off her apartment balcony. It happened two days after her husband's discharge from the hospital. The official police report was suicide, but Seojin didn't believe it. The report stated, "The deceased, who was prone to depression, had several arguments with her husband after his hospital discharge. They were arguing about his home care when, in a rage, she threw herself off the balcony."

The thought that Ina's habitually abusive husband had now murdered her made Seojin choke with rage. But a lover like him was incapable of doing anything. If he had choked the man to death that night, Ina would still be alive. But that was murder, not an easy decision to make. Anyway, he had hesitated, which led to Ina's death, and he had lost his origin of life forever. It wasn't as if he didn't dream about getting revenge, but even if he did, it wouldn't bring Ina back. Only, it was unbearable knowing that her cunning killer got off without punishment. He wanted to somehow destroy the man's life.

Seojin staked out their apartment and waited for her husband. First he would find the man's weak spots by watching where and when he regularly went. The man might even break the law—for example, by frequenting studio apartments for prostitutes. Then Seojin could call the police and make life difficult for him. But as if her husband was still in poor shape, he didn't exert himself. He'd wake up early and go for a walk in the park. At eight-thirty he showed up at an investment firm in the suburbs for work, bought a few items at a convenience store as he left the office, then remained at home until the next day. His apartment lights tended to stay on late into the night.

Once Seojin learned that the man's life was based on such simple patterns, he decided to target his early-morning walk. He wanted to turn up without warning and ask him, "Why the hell did you kill Ina?" But one morning after Seojin actually began trailing him, he wondered if it made any difference whether or not he asked his question and planted fear and guilt in the man. He also feared that the man would threaten or attack him in order to cover up his sins. While Seojin followed the man, feeling conflicted, someone burst out from behind a dawn redwood tree and tackled Ina's husband.

"You fucking murderer!"

Seojin quickly recognized him: the loan shark who'd attacked him from behind the spindle trees. The man climbed on top of Ina's husband and pummeled his face with his bare fists. He beat the husband so badly that it looked as if he might kill him. Within seconds the man's face was a bloody mess. The loan shark's tears as he beat him shocked Seojin, and even more shocking, he repeatedly wailed, "Ina, Ina! Please forgive me. Inaaa!"

The gathering crowd was too alarmed by the loan shark's strength to intervene. Only a passing maintenance worker pried him off the husband. Pinned to the ground by the shoulder, the loan shark pointed at the husband and screamed, "The guy's a murderer! The fucker's killed someone!"

Seojin cautiously left the scene, went to his office, tackled his duties, and ate lunch alone. He'd scheduled afternoon hospital visits, including a stop at the only university hospital in the suburbs. As he passed its emergency center, he wondered if this was where Ina's husband was admitted. He might have suffered serious brain damage after the golf club and then the loan shark. Seojin entered the ER and asked if a patient with brain damage had been admitted that morning. Thanks to a nurse he was friendly with, he easily tracked down the husband's room. The patient looked either asleep or in a coma, and an older woman, probably his mother, sat at his side.

Seojin lied, introducing himself as a work colleague. He asked, "How is he doing?"

She said, "The doctors say that once the intercranial pressure drops, they'll have to operate on him, but the pressure might not drop. He could also be paralyzed, or he could be lying like this forever . . ."

She began to cry. "How did this disaster happen to us?"

"Have they caught the man? Do they know why the man attacked?"

The woman's eyes filled with rage, whose target was probably not the attacker, but her dead daughter-in-law. But she wouldn't reveal that to a stranger.

She continued, "I mean, they said it was an unprovoked attack, but who's ever heard of an unprovoked attack? The bastard should be executed in public." She sighed. "It's his fate. Nothing's going to bring my son back."

When her cell phone rang, she got up to take the call.

Seojin stood over the man and silently looked down at his face. Ina would have made her decision that night. After agonizing, she had chosen Seojin over the loan shark. If she had trusted the loan shark instead, she would still be alive and her husband's life would have ended then. The loan shark would have disposed of the body without a trace and would now be living with Ina. Seojin wondered whether he would have suffered more with Ina dead and gone or alive and the loan shark's lover. It might have been tougher if she were with the loan shark. He despised himself for imagining this with Ina dead, but he couldn't stop. Ina was dead, her husband would soon follow or continue half alive, and the loan shark would go to jail.

He was suddenly overjoyed. He was the only one intact, now and in the future. Happiness overwhelmed him. He had resisted temptation, and even felt proud that he had protected himself from a crisis. Fanciful ideas like the origin of life didn't matter; being alive was what really mattered. Only then did he feel he had truly grown up, as he proudly let go of the sentimental kid who'd read biographies and harbored useless dreams.

He gazed at the man's hand protruding from the sheet, then took the hand in his. It was warm and damp. The man might be squinting out at him, but his face was so bloated that it was difficult to tell. Even if his eyes were open, he probably couldn't recognize anyone. Seojin gripped the man's hand and whispered in his ear, "You woman-beating asshole, you're dying. Or you'll spend the rest of your life on your back like this, pissing and shitting uncontrollably . . . But guess what? I'm alive, I survived. And I love it. I fucking love it."

The mother returned and, seeing Seojin holding her son's hand, thanked him for coming. Seojin slowly let go of the man's hand as if he were a reluctant lover and comforted the mother. "He'll fight back and soon recover. Don't give up."

He left the room and began walking with his bag full of medical supply samples through the hallway, drenched in the smell of ammonia, toward the purchasing manager's office. This, now, must be the new beginning to his life.

MISSING CHILD

olt. The bolt that the mechanic turned aspiring singer was holding while auditioning onstage. While the young man continued singing fervently, Yunseok's focus was on that solid metal part. *If only my hand were holding something. Even a walnut, or a marble ball like the ones they used to sell in stationery stores when I was a kid.* Yunseok stared down at his empty palm.

The store was crowded that summer day. It was just before a national holiday. The three of them—Yunseok, his wife, Mira, and their three-year-old son, Seongmin, who was seated in the shopping cart—took the escalator down to the basement-floor supermarket. It was a scene that would replay in his mind for the rest of his life, but he didn't know it then. A sale was announced over the loudspeaker, and screaming kids raced past the cart. Yunseok had wanted to stay home and watch a baseball game on TV, he really had, but Mira, not he but Mira, had wanted to go grocery shopping.

"You can lie down all you want after you die! Come on. Get up and get the kid ready."

He did what she told him to. Much later, he would often remind Mira that if she had let him finish watching that baseball game, nothing would have happened and they would still be living in their sunny, south-facing apartment. Each time, Mira would blame his careless, indifferent grip, the one that had let go of what was most essential and allowed their entire life to slip away between its fingers. Still, they knew nothing about this yet, and got into their new compact SUV. Their three-year-old son already knew what a supermarket was. He knew that colorful products, free-sample corners where you could eat your fill, awaited him, and chocolates near the checkout counter called to him. Seongmin was excited as soon as he was seated in the car.

Only after parking did Mira realize she'd left the loyalty card at home. She asked Yunseok, "What should we do? Should we just go back?" She always asked first. If Yunseok had said they should go home, she would have said, "Go back when we've come all this way?" He wanted to avoid such useless repetition.

Instead, he said, "You should have had it ready earlier. It's not like the points add up to much. Let's go in."

He put Seongmin into the red shopping cart. The child was so excited that he couldn't stay still. Yunseok pushed the cart behind the other customers, and halted at the mobile phone vendor. He'd wanted to replace his old phone now that his contract had ended, but with long days and late nights at the office, he hadn't had time. "Is this the latest model?" he asked. He rubbed the Motorola that the sales assistant had handed him. It was plastic, but it felt as hard and cold as metal. The clerk continued his sales pitch, saying, "You won't need anything else if you buy this. You can use it to make memos as well as take photos—it's the best all-around phone. Have you used Motorola products before? They have the newest technology." Yunseok's right hand briefly let go of the cart to flip the phone open and examine the screen.

"How much are the monthly payments?" Yunseok asked.

The sales assistant promptly recited the many benefits offered by the phone company if customers signed a contract for twenty-four monthly installments. Yunseok was thinking that he could afford thirty thousand *won* a month. He might even be able to manage forty. The mortgage payments had gone down last month, and his overtime hours had increased. His company's new car model that launched earlier in the year was a hit, and there was a three-month backlog of orders. The factory was operating continuously, with three shifts daily.

"How's this phone?" He turned to his left to get his wife's opinion. But she wasn't there. He turned to the right. He didn't see Seongmin either, who had been sitting in the shopping cart. Had Mira already gone into the supermarket with Seongmin? He returned the cell phone to the clerk and looked for his wife.

As he passed the security gate by the entrance, he heard Mira's voice from behind: "Where are you going?" She was holding her purchases from the cosmetics department. Their eyes met and their facial expressions simultaneously froze. They were looking at each other but seeing nothing. Mira let out a short scream. She dropped the shopping bag. Cotton balls and cleansing cream rolled out. Mira leaned over, collected the items, and ran toward the escalator. Yunseok asked the clerk if he'd seen his son. The clerk shook his head. A three-year-old boy could hardly clamber out of a shopping cart alone and wander off. Someone had taken the cart. Mira looked for their boy around the food-sample corners, running into carts everywhere she went.

Wouldn't there be surveillance cameras?

He followed a security guard into a room with dozens of surveillance monitors, but found that cameras were installed only within the supermarket itself. There wasn't a single one installed to monitor the rented spaces just outside the entrance. A missing child announcement was broadcast three times inside the supermarket, but no one had responded. Just hundreds of carts peacefully rambling like a flock of sheep. Mira wanted to shove between them and shout, *Why aren't any of you listening to the announcement? Don't you have kids, too? This can happen to anyone, can't it?*

Yunseok had looked down at his hand then, too. It had taken only a moment. As if someone had lain in wait, and as soon as he had let go of the handle, silently pulled the cart away and disappeared. Why had Seongmin stayed so quiet? Why hadn't he resisted the stranger?

Ignorance imprisons man in darkness. The couple entered that darkness and began hurting each other. The vanished two to three minutes of their lives existed inside that darkness. He'd say, "You're such a careless mother. You should've said that you were buying makeup." Mira retorted, saying, "Who's the man so crazy about mobile phones that he neglected his son?"

They spent the whole day going from the supermarket to the police station and back. By late evening, they couldn't ignore the ominous feeling solidifying inside them. The sense that they had lost their only son forever.

Ten years later, Yunseok received the phone call. He had just returned from the night shift and assumed that it was the usual prank call. He didn't even get angry anymore. Some—no, many—people enjoyed tormenting others.

The caller asked, "Is your son's name Jo Seongmin?"

"Are you calling about the flyer?" Yunseok tugged off his socks with his free hand.

One got stuck, so he switched hands, pulled the sock off, and tossed it into the corner.

"Flyer? No, I'm not. Could you please confirm your son's name? It is Jo Seongmin, correct?"

"That's correct. Did you see something?"

Papers rustled in the background. It was a noisy place where phones rang incessantly.

"Yes, here it is. You registered your missing child's information on the genetic database, correct?"

Was this a new type of scam?

"Yes, that's right. Seongmin. Jo Seongmin, like the baseball player."

"His name is different, but we have a child with a genetic match."

"A different name?"

"The name was changed, but genes don't lie. It's a 99.99 percent match."

"Where are you calling from again?"

"Daegu."

"Daegu? Where in Daegu?"

"A police station in Daegu. Tomorrow, one of our employees will go up to Suwon with the boy. You will be at home, yes?"

"If it really is Seongmin, I'll drive down right away."

"Oh, there's no need to drive down. These last few days, our employee and your son have developed a good rapport. He'll be going up there anyway for work. We thought we would send them together."

Yunseok hung up and went to the bedroom. Mira's eyes were fixed on the television. He said, "Mira, I just got a call. Seongmin, they say he's alive."

Mira repeated Yunseok's name a few times, gazed baldly at him, then looked back at the TV screen. Yunseok went and held her by the shoulders.

He said, "Honey."

Still her eyes kept rolling to the right like a halibut's. She frowned at Yunseok for blocking the television, so he released her and sprang to his feet. In his room, he hesitated, then made another call.

"Mom, it's me," he said. "I think they've found our Seongmin."

Yunseok's mother, who had spent the past seven years living in a prayer center in the mountains of Gangwon-do, was skeptical.

"No, really, it seems real this time. Seongmin's mom, well, you know her condition. I told her, but . . . No, she understands. I think she understood. I think she's listening, who knows, who knows . . . He said they're bringing him to me . . . I'm not sure. I said it's for real this time. He didn't even mention a reward. I said it's not phishing. I even called again and got the police station . . . Daegu, I don't know either, how he got all the way to Daegu."

He tried to calm his welling emotions by holding the phone away from his face. He breathed deeply.

"Mom, don't cry. You don't have a car. But what should I do now, with our son coming tomorrow and no spare room?"

When he suddenly looked behind him, he didn't see Mira. The front door was ajar. He quickly slipped on his shoes and ran outside. "Mira, Mira," he called.

Though he knew his voice would only drive her farther away, he always called out his wife's name as he looked for her. His wife would scramble up and down the steep, narrow stairs in their neighborhood like a wild goat. The only way to catch her was to take a shortcut. Yunseok had already passed through several front gates of neighbors whom he now knew, climbed onto their roofs lined with clay jars, and headed toward a spring that his wife often stopped at.

He made excuses, saying, "My wife needs air," but their neighbors knew that Mira was sick. That the schizophrenia had worsened.

The social worker who visited once a week had said, "Most likely the shock of your son's loss isn't the main cause. There are many causes."

Yunseok, however, adamantly believed that his wife's illness was a disease of the heart. If they hadn't lost their child, she wouldn't have become like this. When he arrived at the spring, the locals pointed and said, "She just left, the same way she always goes."

Mira was sitting on a hilly slope north of the spring and gazing at downtown Seoul. Yunseok grabbed her arm and, panting, sat next to her.

"Why did you come here again?" he asked. "Do you feel good here?"

She looked suspicious. When he tried holding her hand, her fist shot out and punched him hard in the stomach. His wife was rapidly losing the capacity to sympathize with others. His solar plexus hurt so much he could hardly breathe. He collapsed into a crouch and stayed like that until he was finally able to say, "Let's go. Seongmin's coming."

She said, "Seongmin?"

She was herself again. That was a good and bad sign. When Mira was herself, she was depressed and prickly. Her words and reactions slowed, and her eyes filled with doubt.

"Seongmin? How? Where?"

"He's coming tomorrow. They found him in Daegu."

Mira shook her head. "No, that can't be."

"What do you mean?"

"It's got to be another mistake. How could it be Seongmin? He isn't able to come to us. He isn't able to come and that's why he hasn't come yet. There must be a reason. If he could have come, he would have come earlier."

As Yunseok led Mira back down, the madness overcame her again. She resisted returning home and threw a fit. She bit him and kicked him in the shin. He barely managed to shove her inside the house and follow her in. A huge mound of leaflets lay next to the shoe rack. On each flyer, a photo of Seongmin squinted upward.

The past eleven years of Yunseok's life were summed up in the flyers. He made a living so he could print the flyers, and he stayed healthy in order to distribute them. Each morning, he waited beside the subway and grabbed commuters by the sleeve; on weekends, he visited child protection centers and inquired about his son. He now knew to order extra copies before printers became busy during election season. There were flyers in every corner of his home, in the bathroom, their one bedroom, and stuffed in Mira's worn-out, overflowing handbag. There were so many that it appeared as if a species of insect called "flyer" was slowly devouring the house.

At first, Mira used to take a bundle of flyers and do the rounds with him. Yunseok quit full-time employment at the motor company in order to find their missing son, and Mira also quit the bookstore. If they had known that their son would be missing for nearly eleven years, one of them would have held on to their job. Instead, like an investor trying to recoup stock losses in one big gamble, they risked all to find their son. They lasted a few years by depleting their modest savings, cashing in their insurance policies, then selling their apartment. Three years later, Mira began work as an insurance salesperson, but performed poorly. Customers instinctively detected the scent of repressed, unbearable anxiety. A mother who loses her child is nervous, on edge; people sensed that they would be better prepared for imminent disaster in the company of a bright, energetic salesperson, and more readily signed insurance policies with them. Soon enough, Mira quit insurance work and devoted herself once again to flyer distribution.

Yunseok hopped from job to job, working night security details at construction sites and as a general night guard. He got less than five hours of sleep, but he never complained. As if he were performing a religious ritual, he dutifully distributed flyers each morning and on weekends took their old car across the country. And Mira, Mira thoroughly searched the neighborhood surrounding that supermarket. Every year, Yunseok's friend who ran a photography studio photoshopped a new rendering of Seongmin, one year older than the last. The photoshopped picture had an overly polished, finished look that ended up resembling a funeral portrait. Mira would stare attentively at the children in playgrounds. Seeing her loitering, mothers would call the police, and the police always responded, though the flyers cleared up any misunderstanding. But inevitably, Mira was once nearly charged with child abduction. That day she became convinced that one of the children in the playground was actually Seongmin. She pretended to ask him his name and address, then suddenly embraced him.

A passing yogurt vendor intervened and demanded, "What are you doing?" The vendor called over the apartment building's security guard, and soon the child's mother rushed out to the playground. They released Mira only after Yunseok got on his knees and begged for forgiveness, and promised that they would never see his wife again.

A year after that, Mira returned to that very building, climbed onto the playground slide, and began floating paper airplanes made out of the flyers. She had originally despised anyone who folded the flyer, since it creased her son's face. She had even fought with commuters who crumpled the flyer and threw it away. So Yunseok found her making paper airplanes out of the flyers difficult to believe.

A friend had introduced Mira to Yunseok the same year he'd gotten full-time employment. His first impression was that she was shy and introverted. Mira was raised by her aunt, and as soon as she finished high school, she started working at the bookstore. Looking back, Yunseok saw that something hadn't been right. She was overly sensitive to what others said, or became terrified for no reason. She'd say that the other employees ostracized her, and she was convinced that they insulted her every chance they got. That's unlikely, he said, trying to persuade her, but she remained unconvinced. Mira was his first real girlfriend, and he'd trusted that her ways were typical of a woman's ups and downs.

Two women visited Yunseok, one a police officer and the other a social worker. He peered to see who was behind them, but they were alone; at first he assumed they were evangelizers. He led them into the living-room-cum-kitchen, filled with flyers he'd left in teetering stacks. When their son returned home, he wanted to show him: *Look, this is how your parents lived.*

He said, "Where is my son? Did something happen?"

"Please don't worry. He's in the car."

"Why didn't you come in together?"

The police officer picked up a flyer. "I'm very aware of how desperately you've searched for your son."

Yunseok handed her several flyers with different designs. The social worker inspected them.

"Occasionally, a family will abandon their child, then report him missing. They couldn't afford to raise . . ."

Yunseok had seen such coverage on the news. One woman had abandoned her child and reported him missing in order to remarry, but several years later the child was found through the national genetic database and returned. Only then, the woman confessed and begged for forgiveness. He knew that many were disguised as missing child cases; he now understood why the police station had insisted on escorting Seongmin from Deagu.

He said, "We weren't so bad off then, to abandon our child." He mentioned the name of the motor company he had worked for. "I was a full-time employee, and Seongmin's mom also had a job at the time."

The social worker said, "I didn't mean it that way. If there's been a misunderstanding, I apologize." She added, "Before you meet your son, there is something you should know."

"Is something wrong with him?"

"It could be a problem, or not. It's that . . . you should know how your son's lived all these years."

Had Seongmin's kidnapper chained him to a dog collar in a basement?

Yunseok said, "I'm not sure what it is, but we can gradually figure it out. What's there to worry about when his parents are standing right here. Let me see my son first."

The social worker glanced discreetly around the house.

"Is his mother here? The paperwork shows that he has a mother."

"That's . . . Something came up, but she'll be back very soon."

Yunseok took in the doubtful look exchanged between the two women: *Their son returns after an eleven-year absence and the mother isn't around?*

"Has there been a change in family status or something similar?"

"No, I'm still very much married to Seongmin's birth mother. We put everything into searching for him. She's just out for—"

The impatient police officer cut him off. "Seongmin was kidnapped—let me make that clear. Abducted."

"Of course," Yunseok said. "The shopping cart didn't roll away on its own."

But at the time, the police hadn't ruled out the possibility that the kid had clambered out of the cart on his own, then gotten lost in the busy weekend shopping crowd. The kidnapper hadn't demanded a ransom, which supported their speculation.

"Yes, that's right. But . . ."

"But what?"

"Seongmin had no idea that he was kidnapped."

Yunseok had considered that possibility. Seongmin was three in the Korean counting system, and not yet two in the international counting system, so it made sense.

He asked, "What kind of guy was this kidnapper?"

"It's not a man. She was a woman in her mid-fifties. At the time of the incident, she was in her early forties."

He'd also never imagined the kidnapper was a woman.

"How did you catch her?"

"She wasn't caught—she committed suicide. Jonghyeok found her first and called the emergency number."

"Jonghyeok?"

"Ah, Jonghyeok is Seongmin. When we arrived on the scene we learned she had taken a large dose of antidepressants. The preliminary postmortem report also confirmed suicide. More importantly, we discovered a suicide note. It said she was sorry that she had taken someone else's child but hadn't done a good job raising him. She wanted the boy returned to his family. She'd written down the time and place of the abduction, and they matched the records for your case."

The officer showed Yunseok a photocopy of the note. When he read the line about asking the boy's parents to forgive her, he felt suffocated. Ask only for what makes sense to ask for.

The social worker said soothingly, "Anyway, Seongmin grew up believing that she was his real mother."

Suddenly Yunseok's chin trembled as if his body had gone chilly. He breathed deeply and tried to calm down.

The police officer said, "Your son is in shock. After all, he saw the person he believes is his mother after she killed herself. That alone requires years of therapy, but to make things worse, he learned that he was kidnapped and is now in a state of panic. I kept him with me for a few days, to help stabilize him, but all this is difficult to accept for a kid. I hope you understand how he must be feeling, given that he's experienced great shock and now has to adapt to a new environment."

"Why is my home 'new' when we're his actual parents, the ones who gave him life? There's no need to worry. He's returned to his real family, so he'll soon recover."

"For your environment to dramatically change—that isn't easy, even for a grown-up. I do have one request. Please don't push Seongmin about the past, for now. It's wise to accept him as he is."

As soon as the police officer pulled out her business card, the social worker followed suit. Yunseok learned that the social worker was actually responsible for his district. It was clear that the officer had come up early from Daegu, conferred with the social worker on the handing over of Seongmin, and asked her to please watch out for him.

The front door flew open just as the two women were leaving. They stepped back, surprised by Mira, who ran in whistling, her wrist braceleted with dozens of filthy elastic hair bands. Yunseok leapt forward and grabbed Mira, and Mira, who despised being restrained, screeched like a trapped animal and kicked wildly at him.

"Let me go, let me go, you pig, you filthy son of a bitch. I said let me go!"

Yunseok just managed to calm her, then pushed her into the room.

He smoothed down his rumpled hair and said, "That woman is Seongmin's mother. It was such a shock for her . . ."

As if caught in a dust storm, the two women pursed their lips and squinted toward Mira, then looked at each other. When the officer made her decision and nodded, the social worker said, "We'll bring your son in, then."

Yunseok felt numb. For so long he had lived for this moment alone, so why did he feel this way? He felt no excitement, no emotion. Those two women, his wife slowly going mad, this situation, all of it seemed surreal. Didn't all this surreal evidence mean that the child they would soon bring in was fake? Shouldn't parents instinctively know these things? Was it actually possible for Seongmin to return to them without any signs?

The two women returned, nearly pushing in a boy with dark fuzz under his nose. The boy stopped at the entrance and didn't want to go inside. He looked nothing like the son whom Yunseok had grieved for. He looked nothing like his parents, and shared no resemblance with the face on the flyers they'd handed out for so long. The boy in the flyers had chubby cheeks, earnest eyes, and resembled a TV child actor; the boy in front of Yunseok had long, slanted eyes and a belly.

He looked like a fierce, bad-tempered kid. If Yunseok were to run into him on the street, he wouldn't recognize him. Still, he ran out and took the boy's hand.

"Are you Seongmin? Don't you recognize your dad? It's me, your father."

Seongmin averted his gaze as if he were suppressing his feelings. He kept looking back at the officer. She gently urged him forward and whispered, "Jonghyeok, it's your father. Go on."

The boy took off his basketball shoes and came in with an enormous suitcase. Yunseok signed several forms handed to him without reading them. The officer glanced back several times as she left. One look, and he could tell that the boy had been crying. As soon as the visitors left, Yunseok shut the door behind them and hastily grabbed Seongmin's hand. Still uncomfortable, the boy immediately withdrew it. When Mira emerged and stared suspiciously at them, Yunseok brought Seongmin closer to her, still harboring a last hope that his return would bring back her sanity.

"Seongmin, it's your mom. Do you recognize her?"

He gazed downward, looking perplexed. His eyes darted around as if he'd just been kidnapped. Mira glanced at him, then looked away indifferently. She collapsed to the floor, turned on the television, and sat so close to it that her nose nearly touched the screen. The boy kept sneaking looks at the house. The worn wallpaper stained and spotted with mold. Damp lingerie hanging on a laundry line that cut across the room.

"We didn't always live here. You know, we used to live in a decent apartment. You don't remember? You were already a real talker by then. It was south-facing, with good light."

Yunseok took out the oldest flyer from the closet. "This is you. Do you remember?"

Seongmin looked at his image and mumbled, "Excuse me, but . . ."

"What is it?"

"Where is the bathroom?"

The boy had a strong regional accent, which made him seem even more of a stranger. Yunseok slid open the plastic door; he noticed the boy frown as he entered the narrow, moldy bathroom. Yunseok flushed with embarrassment. He had gotten used to putting life on hold. He had delayed wallpapering the house and doing repairs, even neglected his annual health checkups, until they found Seongmin. Problems piled up. He never had enough time or money; printing costs for flyers and gas prices inevitably rose, never fell.

He waited for Seongmin. He had so much he wanted to share with his son, but he didn't know where to start. He was ready to stay up day and night answering Seongmin's questions, if he would just ask. But Seongmin wasn't interested. Yunseok's stomach throbbed with pain. He'd had intestinal problems for over six months. He couldn't remember when he'd had a good shit. His poop was watery and thin, and half the time he was either constipated or had diarrhea. Sometimes there was blood in his stool. His work colleagues said that stress does that to you, that stress irritates your stomach. Yunseok had gotten used to saying, "This isn't a life worth living."

When the boy didn't emerge for over thirty minutes, Yunseok got a bad feeling. He called, "Hey, Seongmin."

There was no response.

"Seongmin, what are you doing in there?"

Still nothing. Had he run away? Yunseok knew it was impossible, since the bathroom had no windows, but he couldn't help himself. When he shoved open the sliding door, Seongmin was sitting on the toilet, crying with his pants pulled down. As soon as Yunseok went in, he whirled away from him. Yunseok shut the door, but he still heard the murmur of "Mom, Mom" in his ear.

He knew that Seongmin wasn't asking for his birth mother, who was watching cartoons on television. Just then, Seongmin's pleas went from muffled sobs to wailing: "Mom, Mom, Mom!" Yunseok plugged his ears with his fingers.

He went to give his wife a back rub. She giggled and said, "That tickles," and fell to the floor. "Come on, just stay still for a minute," he said, but she was unbearably ticklish. In her attempt to escape, her elbow smashed into his chin. It was so painful he almost cried. Sprawled hangman-style on the floor, Yunseok stared at the scattered bundles of flyers. He took a flyer and looked blankly at the face of the boy he had searched for everywhere for over a decade. The boy in the flyer felt far more familiar to him than the one in the bathroom. There had definitely been a mistake, because a stranger had shown up.

He was reminded of the movie *Back to the Future,* which he'd watched long ago. In it, the main character returns to the past and meets his future mother. In Yunseok's case, it was the opposite situation. Eleven years ago, he was flung abruptly from the past, alone, into the future. In the future he meets his insane wife and his son who believes that Yunseok isn't his father. Neither recognizes Yunseok. He viewed the house again through Seongmin's eyes. Even to Yunseok it was unfamiliar and bizarre: the wallpaper streaks looked like burns, the dusty strips of cellophane everywhere seemed to just barely connect one worn object to the next. *What is my mission in this strange future? What on earth do I have to do?* His duty for over ten years had been clear: to find his missing child. The mission was so clear, so precise, that everyone made way for him.

They had sacrificed their apartment and good jobs, and stopped having sex. The child was the black hole of their life that swallowed everything up. They continued living this way until one day it became normal for them. Even after working all night long, he would feel energetic when, early in the morning, he took his flyers to a subway entrance. He knew the free-newspaper distributor well enough to greet him with a light joke. Factory colleagues who knew his story sometimes relieved him of the more difficult work. For over ten years he had been "the missing child Seongmin's father," but that ended overnight.

If it was true that he hadn't experienced anything like happiness for a single moment, it was also true that he had become used to his misery. *What do I need to do tomorrow?* He had not once seriously considered this. It was always, *If I find Seongmin, if I find Seongmin;* he had never imagined what would happen afterward. If only they found Seongmin, he had believed that even Mira's schizophrenia would disappear.

He somehow endured the unendurable, but what truly felt unbearable was this very moment. He once read an article about a marathon runner who had accidentally taken a shortcut and reached the finish line first, but was stripped of his medal. Whose fault was it when the ending was different from what you'd hoped for? Yunseok thought about this as he listened to the boy's sniffling through the door. When, and why, had everything gone so badly? Was it his wife's fault for wanting to go to the supermarket? Was it his fault for carelessly letting go of the shopping cart? Or his wife's fault for buying cleansing cream? They had resented and blamed each other. Their fights crossed into dangerous territory by blindly probing one another's weaknesses, their subconscious, deepest selves.

"You didn't want children in the first place," Yunseok said to Mira, who had once considered aborting.

Mira screamed, "That's why I'm being punished instead!"

Yunseok criticized Mira in turn, saying, "You're the one who hadn't wanted a baby. What was so important about your work—didn't you say that we should take our time having children?"

After the first few cruel years had passed, years of resignation and cynicism followed. Only the flyer kept them going as a couple. It became their unifying religion and their ritual. The printers they visited monthly became their church, and the flyers were the gospels that helped them forget their earthly struggles and would guide them to heaven. Every day, Mira's condition worsened.

Seongmin hardly spoke. He took a video game console out of his suitcase and played it all day, filling the house with its electronic screeching. Then he sat in one corner of the room, propped up his knees, and buried his face in them for a long time. He spoke only to answer questions, and sometimes retreated to the bathroom to cry. He ate almost nothing prepared for him. At least he ate the instant noodles they bought for him.

Yunseok called his supervisor. "We found Seongmin. Yes,

yes, thank you. It's thanks to all your support. But I should stay home for the time being. The daily log is in the drawer, yes, I think I'll have to stay the night with him. I'm sorry for all the trouble."

Just the thought of the three of them sleeping together in the tiny room left Yunseok at a loss. Seongmin insisted on sleeping in a T-shirt and jeans. As soon as Mira finished splashing around the bathroom and came out in her night-gown, she ran into Seongmin and screamed.

Yunseok said, "It's okay, it's Seongmin, Seongmin," but Mira was so frightened that she fled and crouched in the corner. Seongmin flushed with shame. No matter how many times Yunseok urged her to come to bed, she refused. She looked as if she would flee the house in just her nightgown.

Mira said in a low voice, "Who on earth is that?"

He said, "How many times do I have to tell you that it's Seongmin?"

He gave up trying to persuade her and pulled her force-fully into bed.

"We've got to get your hairpins out if you want to sleep."

At Yunseok's nagging, Mira pouted.

Yunseok turned off the light and lay down. He couldn't fall asleep thanks to his night shifts, and in the new environment, neither could Seongmin. Only Mira slept curled up in a ball as usual.

Yunseok opened his eyes around dawn. Seongmin was toss-ing and turning beside him. Definitely awake.

He said, "Seongmin."

Seongmin stopped moving.

"Did you have your own room, over there?"

"Yes."

"You can just say 'yeah.' Was it big?"

"What?"

"The room, was it big?"

Seongmin merely nodded.

"Did you have a bed?"

Again he only nodded.

"Also a desk?"

"Yes."

Yunseok thought about the kidnapper, the woman who had taken her own life and escaped without punishment. A woman who stole someone else's child and provided him with his own room, bed, and chair. Was chronic depression the cause of the kidnapping? Or the consequence?

Seongmin suddenly spoke up without prodding. "I also had a computer, but the police took it."

"I see."

"Could you find it for me?"

"I'll buy you a new one."

From then on, Seongmin was silent, even when asked a question. Each time Yunseok thought he might be asleep, he heard Seongmin rustling beside him.

Yunseok said, "Let's look for a new place to live. But with your mother the way she is, I'm not sure if anyone will rent to us."

Yunseok tried to fall asleep, but he couldn't. Instead, he spent the night listening to his son's heavy sighs.

Seongmin had arrived on Friday, and he spent Saturday and Sunday in the same state. It was making Yunseok crazy; he was suffocated by the feeling that he had trapped a wild animal. He had no idea what to ask him or how to talk to him.

Officially, he had always been "Seongmin's father," but he had actually never played the role.

At the local mini-mart, Yunseok said to the owner, "I feel like I've become a child abductor."

The owner had been in prison eight times and was a former gang member. He said, "It's 'cause it's a new environment for him. First-timers in the slammer act the same way. Shit, you don't know a soul, you're freaking scared. That's why he's like that—he's scared, freaking scared."

"What do you do in the slammer, to a newbie?"

"They make his life hell till he loses his mind. They roll him up in a blanket and stomp on him, slap him around, shove his head in a bucket," he said enthusiastically, then stopped. "I'm not saying do that to Seongmin. Hell, I got no idea. Anyway, congratulations on getting your son back."

The market owner tucked a sausage snack into Yunseok's bag and said, "For your son."

As he left the store, Yunseok saw his hilly neighborhood anew. It was a neighborhood of multi-unit buildings packed together in cramped alleyways. The cheap houses built by developers had slowly been converted to command high rents. Each house now had two or three separate entrances, and as many as nine people in a single unit. Yunseok's unit wasn't converted only because it was constructed illegally near a public road, so the landowner had trouble changing the zoning. That was why Yunseok and Mira continued living there. But the housing redevelopment board had all but confirmed the neighborhood's demolition, and if that happened, Yunseok's family would be forced to move, since the little compensation left them with few choices. They were pushed out of Seoul, and now they would have to move even farther out.

Money was an issue, but an even bigger problem was finding a landlord who would accept Mira. If he so much as hinted that his wife wasn't quite right in the head, landlords refused them; they believed that a schizophrenic would murder someone or set fire to the house. It didn't matter how many times Yunseok assured them that she was harmless. The real estate agent showing him houses told him to lie, saying, "You can send your wife to a mental ward for a little bit, then bring her back once you move in."

Yunseok became furious because the advice tempted him. He was afraid that he would do just that, despite himself, so he unleashed his anger at the agent instead. If he put Mira in a mental ward, he would leave her there forever. What was more, the superstitions that had sustained him would collapse. He had tricked himself into believing that Seongmin would never return if he sent Mira to the ward, just as he had believed that Mira would fully recover upon Seongmin's return.

But there were other reasons why he couldn't abandon Mira. Others believed that he was burdened with his ill wife, but in truth he depended on her. The same way he handed out flyers daily that wouldn't change anything, he sustained himself with the minimal energy left in his marriage. To him, Mira was like a camel in a caravan. They didn't need to share their goals and hopes. She didn't need to speak, or smile. *Just stay alive till we cross the desert. If not you, my dear, who else would endure this barren hell with me?*

On Monday, Yunseok took Seongmin to school to have his records transferred from Daegu. Seongmin should have been in middle school, but he was still a fifth grader. His abductor had paid a fine, reported him as a newborn, and belatedly legalized his fake birth.

Seongmin's elementary school principal was younger and prettier than Yunseok had expected. She listened to the accompanying social worker's explanation of Seongmin's special circumstances, then approached the matter calmly. She was methodical and courteous, but she didn't seem pleased about being responsible for a troubled kid. Yunseok's working-class shabbiness also probably made her biased. The principal made her feelings clear: A low-income family's child. The father too busy earning a living and the mother too unstable to raise him properly. On top of that, the history of abduction. Take your pick of potential problems. She added, "I'm worried whether he can adapt. If he's going to struggle to adapt anyway, how about sending him up to middle school right away?

"He's the appropriate age, and though his case is unusual, many kids these days also live abroad and return, so there's increased flexibility in the system. Kids' brains are more malleable, so they adapt quickly. But what Seongmin wants is most important."

The principal looked at Seongmin and asked, "What do you want to do? Do you want to start fifth grade with kids two years younger than you, or, even if it's challenging, go to middle school with kids your age?"

As Seongmin hesitated, the social worker cut in. "Won't it be too stressful for him?"

"These days," the principal said, "it's common for students to go over school material at after-school classes beforehand, so most catch up with the curriculum. What do you think,

Seongmin? Did you ever attend any of the after-school study programs in Daegu?"

Seongmin nodded.

"I guessed as much. Most parents have their kids go these days."

The principal's quick glance at Yunseok confused him. Did she want him to make the decision? The social worker and Seongmin also gazed at him. It became clear that they wanted him to decide, but he just couldn't. It was his first time being a school parent.

The principal asked Seongmin, "What do you want to do? That's most important."

Seongmin said cautiously, "I'm not sure."

Yunseok had assumed that the school would administer some kind of basic skills assessment test, that Seongmin would take an authoritative-looking multiple-choice exam and an official choice would be forced on them, but no such test existed. If he made a legal case of it, Seongmin would be allowed to attend the elementary school. His palms became sweaty. The situation was foreign and frustrating. How could he know what a boy wanted with whom he'd never had a real conversation? On top of that, he had no idea whether Seongmin was exceptionally intelligent, or if he was so slow that he didn't know how to do basic math. With no information to go on and with no real relationship with the boy, he had to make a quick decision that could determine Seongmin's fate. He was the legal guardian, but he may as well have been the principal or the social worker.

Yunseok awkwardly put a hand on Seongmin's shoulder. "What do you want?"

Seongmin looked up with disappointed eyes. In the end he said, "I want to go to middle school. Actually, the chairs and desks here are too small for me."

The principal looked delighted. "The decision comes after much thought by the concerned party, so we'll have to respect it. You made a good choice. If you listen carefully in class and review the material thoroughly, you'll quickly catch up."

Then the vice principal came in and whispered into the principal's ear, and her face darkened. The principal took out her cell phone and left to make a call. She quickly returned and whispered something to the vice principal. Then she said to the others, "I have a meeting to attend, but the vice principal will discuss the details with you."

The vice principal's take was different. The board of education had just told her that no matter a child's circumstances, attending middle school without completing elementary school was nearly impossible. In other words, Seongmin had to finish fifth grade first.

Father and son left the principal's office.

Yunseok asked, "Are you hungry? Do you want black bean noodles?"

The boy cautiously asked instead, "Could we get pizza?"

"But you used to like black bean noodles."

"I like noodles," he said, "but I like pizza more."

Pizza was too greasy for Yunseok's taste, so they went to the first-floor Chinese restaurant near their apartment. Pain stabbed his lower belly again. He splurged on a large plate of sweet and sour pork and two bowls of black bean noodles. He ate the pork and the noodles; the boy ate the noodles and didn't even touch the pork.

Yunseok asked, "Did that woman often buy you pizza?"

The boy didn't respond.

"What kind of person was she? She wasn't cruel to you?"

The boy stared reproachfully at Yunseok before averting his eyes. "The same as any other mother, really. Sometimes she gave me a hard time."

"I heard she suffered from depression."

"What is depression?"

"Some signs are being silent all day long, being irritable."

"I'm not sure. Sometimes she was like that. But I was usually at school or after-school lessons."

"Was there a man?"

"A man?"

"A man she was living with."

"Why are you asking me that?"

"Why can't I? The police said that the woman raised you on her own, but didn't you feel that something was wrong? You didn't have a dad, like everyone else."

"She said he'd died. That as soon as she had me, he died in a car accident."

"Then what did she do for a living? She had a job, didn't she?"

"My mom is . . . never mind." As if he'd made a mistake, the boy stayed quiet and weighed Yunseok's reaction.

"It's okay. Tell me."

"She was a nurse, at a university hospital."

A nurse.

"Sir . . ." Seongmin still wouldn't call him "Father."

"What is it?"

"To be honest, I still don't believe what the policewoman said."

"What did she tell you?"

"Was I really kidnapped?"

Yunseok stopped gazing at the ceiling and turned back to Seongmin.

"They've made a mistake," the boy said. "She's not that kind of person, I'm sure of it." He chewed on his lip and held back his tears.

Yunseok ignored this and said, "It's true. The police did say they did a DNA test, and that your DNA matches the DNA record we had for you. You know what DNA is, don't you?"

"I don't know. I don't. How would I know? Do you know?"

I don't know either. I've never seen it or touched it. Before, I wasn't interested in this thing inside me that's innate to all human beings, like the soul that Christians talk about. I started considering genes only after we lost you, after I'd crawled on all fours searching for strands of your hair. I believed that it would help us find you. And because of the test results, you're sitting in front of me right now. But you're a real stranger to me, just like I must be a stranger to you. If the DNA from the hair I finally found on your baby clothes matches the cells scraped from the inside of your mouth, it means that you're the same person, and we have to believe it, we *must* believe it, we've got no choice but to believe it, but why can't we see it with our own eyes?

Yunseok's boss called him. He said he sympathized, but he couldn't keep the night-shift position vacant any longer.

Yunseok sat Seongmin down and told him, "Your dad needs to work nights, so you'll have to take care of your mom."

Seongmin glanced over to where Mira was napping.

"Sometimes she leaves the house," Yunseok said, "but the neighbors will tell you where she went if you ask them. She can't take the bus because she doesn't have a pass. Usually she just walks around, so you'll quickly find her."

"Shouldn't she be in a mental hospital?"

"Your mother is fine."

Seongmin looked confused. His expression said it all: You call that fine?

"It's because of you she's like that, because of the shock of losing you, so she'll recover soon now that you're here, now that our Seongmin is here. Everything's going to be all right, so just keep studying hard."

"I can't study without a computer."

"Things are a little tight right now, but I'll buy you one later."

"I want to go to a cybercafé."

"Then what about your mom?"

"What did you do when I wasn't here?"

"Sometimes I'd lock her in."

"So can I lock the house up, then leave?"

"No. What if your mom's alone when a fire starts?"

"You said that's what you did before."

"We're family, and families have to help each other."

"I told you, I need to use the computer."

Yunseok lost his temper and shouted, "Stop talking about the stupid computer!"

His yelling woke Mira up from her nap. She looked around her. "It's too noisy," she said, and stared at Seongmin.

She said, "Why isn't the kid going back to his house?"

Yunseok said, "It's Seongmin. I'm telling you, it's our Seongmin!"

145

Mira didn't seem to believe him. Yunseok couldn't delay going to work any longer, and once again, as he left, he asked Seongmin to look after his mother.

While Mira continued moving frantically from room to room, Seongmin cautiously tried speaking to her. "Mrs. . . ."

Mira paid no attention to him and continued pacing.

This time, Seongmin said, "Mom."

Mira froze, as if a familiar voice had triggered something inside her brain. She collapsed onto the floor and pulled out flyers from underneath the wardrobe, then looked at them with a long face.

Seongmin gathered up courage and said, "Could you give me some money?"

She stared at him. He became a little bolder and said, "Mom, could you give me some money?"

She backed away from him as he approached.

"You rotten son of a bitch," she cursed. "You lowborn son of a pig, son of a bitch."

She kept cursing at him for no reason, then finally spit at him. She sprang up and opened the fridge. Seongmin watched her shove food into her mouth, then he fled the house. He wandered from alley to alley late into the night. Rumors about a crazy kid who carried a brick in his hand spread throughout his school. That he spoke funny, that he had some kind of southern accent.

Yunseok had to visit the police station three times in less than three months. The last time, Seongmin had fractured a kid's skull with a brick.

"You could have killed him, you crazy kid!" Yunseok

screamed at Seongmin, who was sitting blank-faced in a holding cell. Once they returned home, the little communication they'd had came to an end. Mira's schizophrenia only worsened, with no sign of improvement. Yunseok began thinking daily about suicide. He had long before lost anything resembling a goal in life, and he felt that the possibility of finding meaning had never existed in the first place.

"What would happen if I die?" Yunseok asked Mira.

She was watching TV, and said, "You're being noisy," as she always did.

He even searched for something to hang himself with during his night shift. A construction site was the ideal place to do it. Electrical wire and steel beams were widely available, and there was no one around to stop him. Everything would end once he tied the wire to the beam and let go.

If he hadn't answered the phone that night, the day crew would have discovered his cold corpse the next morning.

It was the police. They had found his wife up in the mountains, and he needed to come to the station to identify the body.

The body laid out in the morgue was indeed Mira. While Seongmin was out at a cybercafé, Mira had broken the lock on the kitchen door, got lost in the mountains, and had an accident. Several days later, when her family showed up for the first time in ages, Yunseok attacked them in the near-empty funeral parlor: "Were you all waiting for Mira to die? Why did you wait till now to show up? Why?"

His father-in-law apologized. When Yunseok asked what he was sorry for, he said for not raising Mira properly. This only made Yunseok angrier.

"Sir, what did Seongmin's mom do? None of it was Mira's fault. If anyone's to blame . . ." He couldn't finish. If anyone was to blame, it was probably Seongmin. For being born, for not crying even when kidnapped, for not helping his mother when they'd barely managed to reunite. But he couldn't bring himself to say any of this, so he stopped. His brother-in-law nearly grabbed Yunseok by the throat and dragged him out of the funeral parlor.

But Yunseok returned later and waited for his son. He had sent dozens of text messages, so Seongmin would certainly know by now that his birth mother was dead, but his son never showed up. In the end, Yunseok managed the funeral alone. He had her cremated and took home the urn with her ashes. It felt as if Mira had somehow wanted to escape this house drowning in flyers.

Seongmin returned just after the funeral procession ended. Only his son's gaunt appearance diminished his father's hurt.

Yunseok asked, "Where were you?"

"Daegu."

"Why Daegu?"

"I wanted to see my mother at the cemetery."

"Mother? Which mother? Your mother died here, not in Daegu. All while you were in a cybercafé."

"Why do you only act like this with me?" Seongmin gazed directly up at him.

"Why do I 'act like this'?"

Seongmin said, "It wasn't my fault. Did I want to be kidnapped? Wasn't my kidnapping your fault, and Mom's? So why do you keep acting like it's my fault?"

"If anyone's to blame, it was your abductor, her alone. That person you call Mom, that crazy woman did this to us."

Seongmin said, "We can't change the past, no matter whose fault it is. So can't we return to living like before?"

"Living like before—how? That woman is dead. You can't go back. You have to live here, with me."

"I hate it here."

"What do you want to do, then?"

Seongmin looked around at the flyers piled everywhere, and the moldy walls, then stared at Yunseok with disgust, making clear that he wanted Yunseok to see his disgust.

"I mean, I really hate it here."

"Then this is what we'll do."

Yunseok had inherited a small plot of land and a store-house in his hometown from his father. He had long before sold the field in his search for Seongmin; all that was left was the storehouse. It could be converted into a small home, and he still had a few relatives in the area. "How would you like to move out there, live off the land?" he asked. "We'll make a fresh start together."

Seongmin said, "Whatever. You'll get to decide in the end anyway."

A few months later, they moved back to Yunseok's hometown. He had a heating system and kitchen installed in the storehouse. Though the structure wasn't zoned for a residence like that, they were so deep in the country, there was no one around to complain. He rented an abandoned mine in the mountains behind the house and began growing mushrooms there. It wasn't exactly successful, but life in the country didn't cost much, and since he could grow basic produce, they were better off than in the city. Seongmin entered middle school, and soon enough started high school. Then one day he left and never came back.

Two years later, a young woman drove into the village, then waited on a wooden bench until Yunseok returned from the mine. She was young, her complexion still dewy, with a trace of pimples across her forehead.

Yunseok said, "Don't I know you? You look familiar."

"I'm Boram, Lee Boram. I used to live just south of here, in Maseok-ri."

She had disappeared from the area around the same time that Seongmin left home. She had been raised by her grandparents, who cried and pestered Yunseok for months to find Boram. When they finally realized that it was useless to try, they stopped coming over.

He said, "What are you doing here, of all places? Where's Seongmin?"

"Actually, I was looking for Seongmin. I thought he might be here."

"No, I haven't heard from him since he left."

Boram dawdled, digging her heels in the dirt.

She said, "I need to get back . . ." Only then, she got to the point. "He—Seongmin—took my money with him. It was all my savings."

Her eyes filled with tears.

He asked, "Was it a lot?"

"To me, yes."

"How much was it?"

"Five million *won*."

He paused.

She said, "I don't understand. Why did Seongmin do that?"

"Humans are a mystery to begin with." Yunseok looked

straight into her face. "I can't give you interest on it, but I'll give you what he took."

He told her to wait, and from the closet withdrew his savings from the mushroom business. Five million *won* was a large sum for a young girl. He withdrew the money from an envelope and slowly counted it out. After repeatedly checking that the sum equaled exactly five million *won,* he hesitated, then added an extra three hundred thousand *won* to the envelope.

But when he went outside, the girl was gone. Her car was gone, too. A baby's car seat was on the bench by the door. A tiny infant gazed up at him, then burst into tears. The girl had tucked a pink slip of paper into the baby's clothes. It read: *The baby is Seongmin's. Seongmin disappeared, and I'm incapable of raising her. Please take good care of her.*

When his right hand grasped the baby's left, the baby's tears halted abruptly and she stared wide-eyed at him. He gently shook the baby's arms from top to bottom. The baby's feet squirmed as if she were ticklish.

Yunseok sat on the bench. Still holding the baby's hands, he continued looking at the small, fragile life that had found him.

THE WRITER

1

Once there was a man in a mental hospital convinced that he was a cob of corn. After extensive therapy and numerous consultations with his doctor, the man only just managed to grasp that he wasn't a cob of corn, and the doctor recommended his discharge. But within days, the man frantically returned to the hospital, frightened out of his wits.

The doctor asked him, "What happened?"

The man said, "The chickens keep chasing me. I almost died of fright."

The man was trembling and kept looking fearfully behind him as if he were still being chased by chickens.

The doctor said soothingly, "You're a human being, not a cob of corn. You're now well enough to understand that."

The patient said, "I might understand. But the chickens don't."

2

Suji had arrived at the café before me and was solving a sudoku puzzle. She enjoyed games where you filled in the blanks, like sudoku or crossword puzzles.

I said, "You've gotten better."

"How'd you know that?"

"I can tell."

Actually, I couldn't.

"Have you eaten?"

"Yeah, I had chicken, teriyaki chicken."

She turned back to the sudoku. After filling in a few blank spaces with numbers, she pushed it aside.

I asked, "How are you these days?"

At my question, Suji began twirling strands of hair around her finger. She did this whenever she didn't want to answer.

"Hard to say. How are you?"

"I was going to say that."

"Shouldn't you be sure?"

"What's wrong with that?"

"You really don't know?"

"I don't."

Her eyes flashed with anger. "You're a shameless, pathetic human being."

I instinctively pulled back. "Sorry," I said.

"Is that all? Sorry?"

"I've got writer's block. What can I do when the words won't come? I've got to write to earn money, and I've got to earn money in order to send you some."

"You think Jjong and I are beggars?"

"Don't jump to conclusions. Who said anything about beggars?"

She gazed out the window and blew her nose.

I asked, "How is Jjong?"

"So you didn't forget her name."

"I said I was sorry, didn't I?"

"When?"

"A little while ago. Anyway, I'm sorry about how things turned out."

She blew her nose again, then looked directly at me.

She said, "My boss is about to eat me alive."

"Why?"

"As soon as he acquired the company, he ordered each editor to submit all their book contracts. Also, he wanted a list of the writers who were paid their advances but haven't delivered a manuscript."

"My name must be on the list."

She said, "Probably at the very top."

"Where'd you say the new publisher's from?"

"From Wall Street."

"Why'd such a hotshot acquire a snot-sized publishing house in Korea?" I asked.

"We're not that small a company."

"That so?"

"He wants to run it American-style."

"So if I don't turn in my manuscript, he'll blindfold me and take me to Guantánamo?"

"First he'll issue an ultimatum, and if you don't produce, he'll sue."

"What? He'll sue? Is that why he sent you, to deliver the ultimatum? Does he have any clue that we were once hitched?"

"He does. That kind of stuff doesn't seem to matter in America. Or maybe he thinks that I'll get through to you fastest."

"I hate America. Those imperialists!"

"I don't like the country either."

"I despise it."

"What are you going to do? Are you going to cough up the advance? Or do you want to negotiate a new deadline?"

"And if I don't do either?"

"Then our in-house lawyer will give you a call."

"When did the publishing world become so brutal?"

Suji said, "Mansu . . ."

She suddenly looked somber. She always called me this when a serious subject—money—came up.

"I hadn't planned on bringing this up."

"Then don't. Preferably forever."

"I won't ask for the overdue alimony payments. If—"

"If?"

"Well, Jjong—I don't know all the details, but your daughter Jjong apparently applied on her own initiative to some American universities."

"Don't we have universities in Korea? Anyway, so?"

"They contacted us."

"The bitter taste of failure can teach you a lot at her age. Tell her not to be too discouraged."

"UCLA, Iowa, Pennsylvania State University, and about

two others whose names I don't remember. Anyway, believe it or not, five universities sent her acceptances."

"That's truly amazing. How did we get such a brilliant daughter when neither of us is all that bright?"

"There's no scholarship money. She says it's normal for undergraduate programs."

"Can I smoke in here?"

"Don't change the subject."

"I knew it. It didn't make sense. I heard that the good universities give scholarships, even for undergrad."

"Jjong said that she only applied to universities with low tuition fees on purpose."

"Does that mean she could've gone to the pricy private ones like Stanford, too?"

"If she'd had a more responsible dad, she would've applied to those schools, too."

"Why does everything end up being my fault?"

"Now it all depends on you," Suji stated solemnly.

I made a dismissive gesture. "When did writers ever have any money? You already know I've gone through the advance. Asking, when you know my situation. I'm drowning in debt."

"Fine. Then you tell Jjong. Tell her it's a real shame, but she has to give up because her parents don't have the money. I can't tell her."

"Why's she so shrewd?" I asked. "Where does a high school student get the idea that she has to go to college in America? Is it watching too many American TV shows? When we were young, we were just so grateful if our parents sent us to a college in Seoul."

Jjong had had a will of iron since she was young, and she

couldn't stand losing. She would pull all-nighters studying in elementary school, and would wail if she so much as lost playing a board game. The luckiest moment of my life was when her mother and I separated, and little Jjong chose her mother and left me.

I added, "It looks like I'll be a pauper soon, once the hot-shot Wall Street president sues me, so how could I cover her tuition? Does that make any sense?"

Suji sighed and lowered her eyes.

"Jjong said to loan her the first semester's tuition and dorm housing." Suji's voice faltered. "She—she wants a loan. And she said she'll pull together the rest somehow. Just a kid, but she picks up on everything."

Suji seemed a blink away from crying.

I tried calming her down right away. "Can't you help her? Doesn't Wall Street pay you a salary?"

"You know what publishing is like."

"All right, all right. Then what should I do?"

"Write that novel quickly. There's no other way. It's the only thing you know how to do to make good money. I'll make things right with the boss. You know it's been ages since you've had a novel out. If you publish one now, it should do well. I'll cobble something together for the first semester's tuition, then you find a way to manage the rest from there."

"Isn't there another editor in the house besides you? What kind of publisher sends you to collect a manuscript from your ex-husband?"

Suji tried to pacify me. "Stop being angry and just think about it. You're a good writer. You'll be recreating the glory of your debut. Stop running away and let yourself really write. This could become a good opportunity."

"I've never run away and I've never held back while writing. I've given it my best every single time!"

"True, true. That's true," Suji agreed halfheartedly. "So, any chance you're working on something right now?"

This is her playing the role of editor.

"Well. I've got some words down, but it's still a secret."

"It must be pretty good if it's a secret."

"I won't know till I'm done. Meanwhile, I'm working hard."

All writers tell their editors the same lie.

"What is it? I'll keep it to myself."

All editors pretend they believe what their writers say.

"It's about a traveling circus troupe during the Japanese colonial period, told in the style of Latin American magical realism."

I made up whatever came to me.

It's good to drop in magical realism or surrealism when you're talking to your editor about a book. That way, you get the editor's imagination going, and soon enough they've taken to your story.

She said, "It sounds fascinating!"

I've even won over my ex-wife. This is precisely the magical and real power of magical realism.

"But here's the thing—I heard that the last surviving member of the circus troupe lives in New York. I need to interview him, but it's not like New York is next door, and it's outrageously expensive. Plus, there's no guarantee I'll actually find him . . . So I'm not making any progress. Even if it is magical realism, it still has to be supported by facts."

Her eyes flashing, she leaned over the table.

"My boss has a studio apartment in Manhattan. He bought it planning to go back and forth, but it's empty right now since he's in Seoul. Should I ask for you? If he knows you'd be writing your novel there, he'd gladly loan it to you."

"You seem to know a lot about your boss."

"So will you go or not?"

"Don't you have to ask him first?"

"First tell me what you think."

"It's as if it's your house."

"Are you going to keep this up?"

"All right, I'll go. I'll go."

"You're doing the right thing. It's a good opportunity."

"But isn't your boss married?"

"You're doing it again. Being pathetic."

"At least tell me that much. I'm so curious I can barely stand it. Is he married?"

"They're separated."

"You sure it's not, 'He says they're separated'?"

"Don't pick at my words."

"Separated . . . That's what they all say."

This last comment got to her.

"Don't you feel ashamed when you think about Jjong? How can you say that when you aren't even a decent father?"

"All right, all right, sorry. Okay, I am kind of pathetic. Fine. Then how about this. Could you politely ask your most respected boss for a free few months' loan of his amazing New York apartment, in the heart of Manhattan, to a pitiful writer in a slump who can't even meet his submission deadline? I'll most gratefully work on my novel and complete it by the due date, so please entreat him in my place to forgive me for the previous breach of contract."

"You're being a pain."

"Okay."

Suji drove back to work, but I stayed in the café. Whenever I met her, I strangely found myself relapsing into my immature past self. I act like a baby, provoke her, beg for consolation. I'm not a cob of corn anymore, truly not a cob of corn, but since Suji doesn't realize this, the fact that I'm no longer a cob of corn doesn't matter one iota. I looked up as I left the café. All I saw in the overcast sky was a swarm of plump pigeons.

3

I have two friends who both have sex partners. One teaches philosophy at a university while writing poetry, and the other writes poetry while running a café. But the café manager writes far more complex poems than the philosophy professor. Anyway, they despise each other. We used to go bar hopping together, but that time's long past. Once I asked my philosophy friend about his sex partner, and he answered:

"Some people believe there's an exchange between sex partners. I don't agree. Exchange? Of what? Just like countries at war don't exchange war, or baduk players don't exchange baduk, sex isn't something sex partners exchange. I don't meet her for an exchange, but so that I can waste. Together, we use up our time and our energy. But that's the concept behind sex: positive waste. That heavy concept of 'to have sex' —I discard it the way a dump truck does sand, and I return home feeling lighter. The way Wittgenstein would see it, we're sharing a box called 'sex partner.' It doesn't matter what's inside the box, as we've agreed that it's called 'sex partner.' We don't open the box. So long as we don't take off the lid, we're safe."

The woman that Philosophy is *wasting concepts* with is Café's wife.

I asked, "How often do you two meet a month?"

He thought for a moment, then shook his head. "I can't say exactly. Sometimes we meet every week, other times we don't see each other the whole month. Why're you asking?"

"You know I'm a Proustian kind of novelist, curious about everything. But once a month? When that day approaches, you must stink like a city with its sanitation workers on strike, since the concept of 'to have sex' must have piled up in your venerable mind."

Philosophy spun his beer glass in his hand. He did this when he was in a foul mood. He did this for a while, then said sarcastically, "Then what about you? How do you take care of the concept?"

"I don't take care of a concept, but the fluids. In all sorts of ways. We fiction writers, we need to be realistic."

"Do you really think it's that simple?" he objected. "In your work you actually begin with a concept, then add the flesh of the real to it. You set out with an idea, then add flesh. So no matter what you say, you also first have to deal with a concept."

"Novels don't work that way. They're extremely concrete. When the heart moves, the mind obeys. We're built differently from poets or critics. We're the marines of literature, its manual laborers and butcher shop owners."

He said, "I've got a bad feeling about your certainty."

Cynical. Definitely a philosopher.

•

I once asked my café friend, "What do you call your girl?"

My friend, who now resembled the retired pro wrestler he really was, became a little shy when he talked about girls.

He said, "To be honest, we use nicknames for each other. I've probably used over a hundred nicknames on her, 'cause we call each other a new name every time we meet. The more meaningless the name, the better. I've called her anything from 'my chair with a broken leg' to 'my very empty steamed bun.'"

"Have you ever called her 'sex partner,' even as a joke? Or at least abbreviated, like 'sexpa'?"

"Some moms these days apparently call their sons 'Son.' It makes me uneasy every single time—it's as if the mom has crossed some line. Once she calls her son 'Son,' any form of buffer zone between the two disappears. It's the same for sex partners. What I mean is, if you want to grill something in a frying pan, you've got to first surround it with cooking oil. That way, they won't stick to each other."

"Wait a minute. That girl, what did you say she does for a living again?"

"I don't think I've ever mentioned it to you."

Leading questions are my specialty, but they don't work so well on someone who's used to them.

"All right. Then I'll ask again. What's she do for a living?"

"She's an army officer."

"Really?"

"I drive to Gangwon-do every weekend, since she's stationed near the border. It'd be problematic for rumors to spread in such a small neighborhood, so she changes out of uniform and disguises herself with makeup, then heads out to a nearby city, farther south from the border, for our rendezvous."

"I see."

"I've had a thing for girls in uniform since I was young."
He became even more embarrassed.

"Is the phrase 'girls in uniform' a type of cooking oil?"

"Yeah. That's why I can be 'the guy into girls in uniform.'
Of course, since you're a fiction writer, you got it right away."

"Isn't she in civilian clothes when you're together?"

"Civilian clothes, that's right. But the fact that she has
to 'get changed' in order to meet me, that gets me excited.
Other girls 'get dressed' to meet a guy, but she's got to 'change
clothes' to meet me."

Café, rattling on and drunk on his own words, doesn't
know that his wife is sleeping with Philosophy and discard-
ing the heavy concept of "to have sex" with him. Since ancient
times, the husband has been the last to know. Likewise, Café's
wife and Philosophy don't know that Café is sharing cooking
oil in a frying pan with a female officer. They just believe that
Café is wild about fishing.

4

Suji called, saying that her boss wanted to meet me.

I asked, "Are you coming together?"

She said, "No, he wants to see you alone."

When we met, her boss was wearing a well-fitted navy
blazer, white slacks, rust-colored loafers. He reminded me of
a kid from the Gangnam district with well-off parents, the
kind more likely to run a golf shop than a publishing firm. He
had large eyes but a small nose and narrow lips, and deep dark
circles under his eyes that gave him a raccoon look.

We settled into a bar in the Samcheong neighborhood and drank Bordeaux with a platter of ham and cheese. We brought up the typical topics, from the publishing industry slump to the chaotic political situation in Korea, then dropped them.

Finally he said, "Mr. Bak."

"Yes?"

"I'll be truthful. I'm a hardcore fan."

Perhaps. I didn't respond and just smiled ambiguously. He then pulled out a shopping bag and placed it on the table.

"What's this?" I asked.

"Copies of your books, of course. I brought them for you to sign."

One glance told me that it was the complete collection of my books, from my debut to my latest. Suji had probably packed them up for him. I didn't let my guard down and checked the copyright page of a few he pulled out. Unexpectedly, they were all first print runs.

"Are these all really first editions?"

"Yes. I told you, I'm a real fan."

Raccoon looked embarrassed as he scratched at his hair. I began signing them one at a time. As he'd said, each was a first edition. Even more intriguing was that the margins of the pages were crammed with notes. When I tried to get a better look, he seemed startled and made a dismissive wave.

"Please don't look. You get lonely living in a foreign land. I get all sorts of thoughts whenever I read your work, and I jot them down each time so I won't forget, so these precious books are all marked up with my scribbles."

"Oh, so you put down your reactions into the margins."

"No, nothing like that. It's impertinent of me, but I tend

to imagine how I would have written it, something like that. I've had the habit of making up stories as I read novels since I was a kid."

"You haven't tried writing any yourself?"

"I wouldn't dare. All I do is more or less think up a plot, that level."

"Did you buy all the first editions while you were in America?"

"Not all of them. Some I bought in Korea. When I was in New York, a friend who knew I liked your work would send me your new books each time one was published."

"You have good friends."

I must have signed at least a dozen books. No writer dislikes a reader who has collected first editions of all his books, then filled page after page with notes. And if that very reader has just bought out a publishing firm, there was nothing more a writer could ask for.

"Mr. Bak, you've no idea how it comforted me, while living so far away, to know that such a writer existed in my lifetime."

"Well, thank you."

I hadn't heard such high praise in years, so I was bewildered. He began chatting about my work. But here's this: a writer doesn't remember every single line he's written, and his readers also forget, or misremember. As a result, when a writer and a reader meet and talk about books together, the atmosphere eventually becomes rather awkward. By now I was somewhat used to these situations, but this conversation was especially confusing. Since he'd created alternate plot lines in the margins, he'd come to mistake parts of his story for mine. Or I could be the one remembering incorrectly. I no longer let it bother me. I mean, does the way a reader remembers my work really affect me?

He said, "From what Ms. Lee tells me" — he meant Suji — "you're working on a new novel."

"Oh, that? It's still in the early stages."

"I heard that —"

"Yes, I'm writing a book about a traveling circus troupe during the Japanese occupation."

"That's marvelous! Actually, as soon as I heard this from Ms. Lee, I snapped my fingers and said, 'That's it! A traveling circus troupe!'"

He was barely able to stay in his seat as he spoke. Somehow that made me anxious.

I said, "Who would be interested in a traveling circus story? I don't think it'd sell so well."

"It doesn't matter. Whether it sells or not, some books just have to be published. But that doesn't mean we wouldn't work hard to sell it. We'll do our utmost to make sure your reputation isn't tarnished. And even if it doesn't sell — no, even if the firm goes bankrupt because of your book — I have to publish it."

"It would be terrible if you went bankrupt."

"Did you hear that I worked at Goldman Sachs?"

"I only heard that you worked on Wall Street."

"I worked at Goldman Sachs, the investment firm of investment firms. It's a long story. My father was against me dating the woman I loved. You see, her family was poor. He was unconditionally opposed to us, so I took her with me to America with nothing but a vague idea to eventually return with money. And after five years, I came home with three billion *won* in my pocket."

"Three billion!?"

"On the surface, banks like Goldman Sachs look flashy. Most imagine bankers in white shirts and Armani suits sitting behind mahogany desks as they meet clients. Hah! We call those guys soldiers. They're the ants at the very bottom who invest other people's money. We also call them galley slaves. When the Goldman Sachs people make a toast, you know what they say?"

"What?"

"They say, 'To OPM.'"

"What does that mean?"

"To other people's money. Wall Street bankers do everything with other people's money. They invest, build buildings, and eat with other people's money. People who invest their own money and take on the risk themselves are fools."

"OPM, you say."

"But here's the thing. At the heart of the institution are the executive board members who invest Goldman Sachs's money. These guys show up for work in Gap T-shirts and Levi's, and wolf down burgers while they tap away at the keyboard, but they're the ones that the corporation has absolute faith in. I was one of them."

"Wow, that's impressive."

"I'm telling you all this because you are our firm's main asset and its most important human resource. What I mean is, you're no galley slave to us. When it comes to publishing your book, I don't need OPM. I'm willing to lose my entire net worth to publish you."

"But, as you know, my books haven't been doing so well lately—"

"Please stop, please. Wasn't that when the publishing company was under the former publisher? I'm a professional manager. I learned exactly one thing while on Wall Street. Do you know what that is?"

"OPM?"

"No!" he said in English and shook his head vigorously.

He added, "The bottom line is this: a company's worth lies in its people. When I first scouted the Korean market to take over a publishing company, there were several options. Many firms were in better financial shape and had a strong backlist, but as soon as I saw your name, I made my decision. Why? If I buy this company, I told myself, I would be this author's—"

As if he were taking an oath, he placed his hand on the pile of books.

"—companion, since I'd be the publisher of his books. And for a mere two billion *won*! I couldn't believe it."

"Well, I don't know," I said. "It is quite a bit of money . . ."

"Money's no issue. I was determined to do something I cared about before it was too late. What's the most dignified work a business grunt who loves books, literature, and writers, but has no talent or ability, can do? Isn't this my best option? Am I wrong?"

He sprayed spittle on my face as he spoke.

"Mr. Bak," he added.

"Yes?"

"Please, just write me one novel. I'll wait without fail until the day your precious words fill the bookstores, my undeserving name printed inside its covers."

"I understand. I'll do my best."

His enthusiasm was contagious, and before I knew it I had agreed.

He drank some ice water and asked, "When will you depart for New York?"

"New York?"

"You said that's where the last surviving member of the circus troupe lives, so you needed to go for research."

"Oh, yes. I'm thinking of leaving at the end of the month."

"I'm asking because I need to let the apartment manager know. In case you experience any discomfort while you're writing there."

He handed me a business card. "If you get in touch with him, he'll take care of anything that comes up."

He added, "It's in a prime location. The neighborhood's near the financial district, and you can walk to Wall Street, SoHo, and the East Village. It's an apartment in a stately, traditional brownstone. It's got walnut molding, a wood-burning fireplace. The kind of place that's perfect for writing a book. There are also many restaurants nearby, so it'll be convenient."

We left the wine bar. We were heading elsewhere for beer, as he had suggested, when his phone rang. He answered, his face turning grave as he spoke. Then he excused himself, saying, "My son's suddenly feeling ill. What should we do?"

"You should go," I said. "We can always meet another time."

The boss hailed a taxi and quickly left. Alone, I stared into space. I didn't feel like going home, so I called my philosophy friend.

I said, "It's me."

"Where are you?"

"In the Samcheong area."

"What're you up to?"

"I met the publisher, and—"

"What'd he say?"

"That he's a hardcore fan of mine."

"It's the same old strategy."

"Maybe."

"Anything between him and Suji?"

"I don't think so."

"Did you ask him?"

"How could I ask that?"

"Then how do you know?"

"I can just tell. He's not that kind of person."

"Where is he now?"

"His son got sick, so he went home."

"What kind of fan is that?"

"His son is sick, what else could he do? He got a call."

"So? Did you agree to go to New York?"

"Yeah."

"So that's how it ended," he said, sounding disappointed.

"How about a beer?" I asked.

"I can't. I have to be up early."

"All right. Get some sleep."

I tried to hail a cab, but it proved difficult. Around five cabs passed with customers on board. That's when I called Suji.

After a long stretch, she picked up. I asked, "Where are you?"

"I was just about to leave."

"Where, at this time of night?"

"What are you, my husband?"

"You're right. It's none of my business."

"By the way, how did the meeting go?"

"Why're you using the past tense?"

"What are you talking about?"

"You said, 'How did the meeting go?' Not 'Are you meeting him?' I didn't say we'd parted ways."

"Did I? Then are you still with him?"

Suji had a naïve side to her. She was bad at lying.

"No, he's gone. He said his kid's sick."

"Is that so?"

"To be accurate, his kid conveniently got sick just after the first bar and before we got to the second."

"You're so sarcastic."

"Clever, you mean."

She said nothing.

"Suji."

"What?" she said, her voice rising sharply.

"Nothing."

"Tell me."

"Why's your boss so set on my manuscript?"

"He says he likes your novels."

"I met him assuming he only cared about money, but then he didn't seem that way. But I thought about it after he left and realized he seems exactly like a guy who only cares about money. So why would a guy who only cares about money want my novel that won't sell well?"

"That man has a sixth sense for making money. You heard he left home penniless and came back with three billion *won*. Just trust him and give him your manuscript. You never know, it may do well."

"You think I should?"

"Please let me off here," I heard her say to a cab driver. She added, "I've got to go now. Let's talk again tomorrow."

I left Samcheong imagining my ex-wife and her boss in various sex positions.

5

A few days later, I met my philosophy friend for a beer. After hearing what Suji and I had talked about, he asked, "So, will you go to New York?"

I shook my head. "No."

"But you said you were going."

"Only to get Suji off my back. You know how stubborn she can be."

"Girls who know what they want are always stubborn."

"That so?"

"So why won't you go to New York?"

"Listen. Here's my dilemma. Let's say I go to New York and write a hell of a novel."

"Easier said than done."

"I'm just hypothesizing. Aren't you a philosopher? You don't know what a hypothesis is? An *if*, an *if*."

"Okay, okay. So?"

"Thanks to the novel I'd torture myself to write, Suji will be regarded as a fantastic editor at work, and the man she's sleeping with will make a lot of money, right?"

"Wait! What if Suji and her boss don't have that kind of relationship?"

"They do. I'm sure of it," I said.

"Really?"

"I've got a sixth sense for these things."

"Why would a guy who's made a fortune on Wall Street want to date a divorced mom in her forties?"

I said, "Why would someone like you have sex with your friend's wife, out of all the women in the world?"

"That asshole isn't my friend. And we're not having sex. I told you, we're disposing of the concept of sex together."

My friend, this is why no one cares about philosophy.

"Anyway, if the novel I bust my ass writing sells well, it'd only fatten my ex-wife and her lover's coffers."

"Probably true."

"But if it doesn't sell, they'll probably talk crap about me over drinks. They'll say things like, 'His writing career is over. I was right to divorce him. He calls *that* a novel? How will he survive the twenty-first century writing such old-fashioned books?' Et cetera."

"Don't beat yourself up."

"Beat myself up? I told you, all of this is hypothetical! If, if, if!"

"It is a real dilemma. You write a good book, it's a predicament. You write a bad book, an absolute embarrassment."

"That's why not writing it is the best solution."

"But now you have to write it. Won't that Goldman Sachs tightwad sue you?"

"He'll probably sue me for the advance. A real Shylock!"

"He could also get you for fraud."

"Fraud? What kind of fraud did I commit?"

"He can claim it's fraud because you had no intention to write the book yet you accepted a large advance. If it's fraud, it becomes a criminal case. So he'll first claim fraud, then simultaneously proceed with a civil suit."

"Then the publishing industry will bury the bastard alive. Who's going to sign with a publishing company that sues one of its own writers for fraud?"

"I still think he'll at least proceed with a civil suit."

"That asshole is clearly jealous of my talent. In order to win over Suji, he has to expose me as incompetent. That's why he deliberately sent Suji to me. He set a trap. What a coward. Does he think I'm going to just sit there and take it?"

He asked, "Is Suji really that amazing a woman?"

I said, "Well, he's probably blinded by love."

"Any brilliant ideas?"

"I'm thinking of meeting him again and coming to an agreement."

"Will he agree to it?"

"He will."

"But wait. Isn't writing a book ultimately good for the writer? Whatever happens behind the scenes, it's your book once it's out in the world."

"This is why you're a capitalist tool."

"I teach at a public university—it's the nation that's supporting me. And I self-publish my poetry books."

"Aren't you lucky."

"That's right," he said. "Anyway, what're you going to say after meeting the publisher? Tell him you can't do it?"

"I'll make him an offer he can't refuse."

"So now you're the Godfather?"

"Yeah."

"What's the offer he can't refuse?"

"I'll tell him that I'll turn a blind eye on his affair with Suji. That I'll steer clear of Suji and be eternally absent from family events, even from Jjong's wedding. I'll do all this so long as he calls off the book contract. I'll say I truly don't have a whisker of interest in publishing a book with his firm—and if I had to, I'd sooner give up the pen forever."

"Isn't disappearing from Suji and Jjong's life what you want anyway? You hate Suji, and you're not so happy with Jjong, either. You think the man won't know this? It's a deal far too easy for him to refuse."

"Would he really know that?"

"Why wouldn't he? He'd know if he's close to Suji, and if there's really nothing going on between them, you'd be way off. I mean, you have no evidence that he likes Suji."

"True."

"Then how about this instead?"

"What?"

"Write an unintelligible, chaotic book that's unpublishable. Write something like James Joyce's *Ulysses*. A difficult book, one around a thousand pages long, without a clear plot line or a recognizable subject."

"*Ulysses* has a plot and a concrete subject."

"To be honest, I haven't read it. What's it about?"

"It's about a petty middle-aged guy and his messy sexual fantasies."

"Sounds similar to Kubrick's *Eyes Wide Shut*."

"You're right. That's the whole story right there. The American prosecutor who claimed that *Ulysses* was obscene knew what he was doing. Sometimes people who have nothing to do with literature see right into a writer's inner self."

"Which is why I'm saying write something like *Ulysses*. If it's lewd, even better. If all goes well, he might land in jail for publishing it."

"*Ulysses* isn't the kind of novel all that easy to write."

"So you have to write it badly. It's easy to write badly, isn't it?"

"Even that's not easy—at least for a writer like me, whose skills have reached a certain level."

He ignored my protests and said, "You'll be reversing the situation and creating a major dilemma for the man. It'll be an underdog victory. And as long as you submit the manuscript, you'll be fulfilling your contract."

"Um, right, since it'll be a near-thousand-page, chaotic, lewd, experimental mess."

"That's it! He'll probably never be able to publish it. If he does, he'll be in trouble. I hear the price of paper's gone up a lot lately."

Philosophy was so excited by the idea, he started clapping. We made a toast. He emphasized again that writing an abstruse, fragmented, filthy novel that put the publisher in a difficult position was a great idea.

He added, "What's more, you won't need to go to New York."

As I watched him obsess over New York, I suddenly decided that I had to go. Why not just go and write it there?

6

The publisher's apartment wasn't quite as he had promised, "a stately, traditional brownstone." The interior was worn and gloomy, and it hadn't been maintained. Instead of a lovely garden and bright sunlight pouring into the apartment's only two windows, the view was of an enormous ventilator. When

I opened a window, a cacophony like General Rommel's army and summer heat invaded the room.

And the neighborhood. The publisher's neighborhood "near the financial district" was actually Chinatown. A cluster of fishmongers stood a mere block away, and next to them several stores sold cheap Chinese counterfeit goods. The streets brimmed with sludge from the food waste set out by local restaurants; the stench worsened in the hot, humid weather. A homeless shelter sat adjacent to the apartment. Someone told me that the city government had purchased the shelter that an individual once ran as a charity.

Now that I was here, I decided to enjoy myself, and kept a frantic pace for no reason, visiting museums and bookstores, but that didn't last long. At night the whirring ventilation system gave me nightmares. In one of them, I rode a whirring, violently pitching ferry to a distant land I'd never visited, only to discover that I didn't have my passport. It became impossible to write in the apartment so I went to some cafés nearby, but there were few places in Manhattan where you could write in peace.

My vow to cause the publisher trouble by writing a thousand-page, incomprehensible novel seemed an increasingly meaningless, reckless idea. My days of drinking wine by the bottle and battling the ventilation system's extreme noise hit a nadir when two plump rats emerged late at night. I was dreaming about fighting a bear that had suddenly appeared on the pitching ferry's deck when I woke up to a rat on my chest, gazing at me. The rat rambled toward my feet. Immediately, another one followed the same path. I flew upright, turned on the standing lamp, and watched the rats disappear into the closet. Maybe it was just my hangover—my head was thundering. The clock showed a little after three a.m.

I rummaged around the apartment for painkillers and ended up opening the bedside drawer. Inside was a box of condoms, an eye mask, and a loaded gun. When you hold a loaded gun, you can feel its weight. It's the same feeling as entering an old European cathedral. A feeling deep in your bones, as if you're going from one world to another, crossing the border between life and death, sex and interiority. The grip was engraved with the logo *GLOCK GmbH*. I recalled that a Glock was one of the guns used in the Virginia Tech shooting, as well as the shooting of US Representative Gabrielle Giffords in Tucson. It's said that Saddam Hussein was also carrying a Glock on the day he was captured. I put the gun back. It was time to reconsider what I knew about the publisher. I added another hashtag to my mental file on him: #publisher #Wall Street #raccoon #loadedpistol. He was no longer merely a weak raccoon who'd had some luck on Wall Street.

Was there any chance that the publisher intended to encourage my suicide? Had he locked me up in a stuffy studio, where sleep was impossible without the help of alcohol, to pressure me with the aid of a contract, a lawyer, and my ex-wife? "Writer Bak Mansu, Gunshot Suicide in Manhattan Apartment." "Writing Slump Led to Signs of Depression." The greatest beneficiary? The publisher. The bookstores would set up a special display to commemorate me, and for a while my book sales would skyrocket. Jjong would inherit the rights to my books. My shrewd daughter would use that money toward tuition. I vowed never to do something that would solely benefit others. But minutes later, I realized I was thinking about shooting myself again.

I told myself: Let's pack and return to Seoul. Even if I have to beg other publishers, let's pay back Suji's publisher. First, I must live. If I stay here, I won't reach the end of my last days. I was mulling these things over breakfast when the front door flew open and a woman in her mid-thirties dragged in a large suitcase. She was so good-looking that any ordinary guy would instantly feel shy.

I asked, "Who are you?"

She looked even more alarmed than I did. Her bag seemed to faint as it collapsed diagonally with a thud.

She asked, "And who are you?"

I said, "Who gave you the keys?"

"Who gave me the keys? They're mine."

"I'm the fiction writer Bak Mansu."

Maybe she wasn't interested in literature, as she had no idea who I was.

I added, "From what I know, my publisher owns the apartment."

As if she only now understood the situation, she set the bag upright.

"Don't just stand there," she said. "Please help me with my bag."

I did as she asked, took the bag and dragged it in.

The woman mentioned the publisher by name, then said, "Why would that man loan you someone else's apartment?"

She told me she was the publisher's wife, now separated from him. I added another tag to my mental file on him: #publisher #Wall Street #raccoon #loadedpistol #beautifulwoman.

I said, "Actually, I was just about to finish up and leave."

"Oh, is that right?" She crossed her arms and stared at me as if expecting me to pack up and go.

I said, "Ah, I didn't mean I was leaving immediately. I meant I was thinking of leaving for Seoul in the next few days."

"Then what should we do? There's only one bed, and no real sofa."

"That's true."

"You can't just say 'That's true.' This *is* my house, after all." She frowned, then pulled out her cell phone. Her profile was even more stunning. Her beauty was far from ordinary; I wondered if she was a former model. Why on earth would the publisher leave his wife and date a hick like Suji?

The woman went on to have a heated discussion on the phone with the publisher. Their first round, over who owned the apartment, ended; then, over the next half hour, they attacked one another's personality and general conduct. I didn't want to eavesdrop, but I ended up overhearing everything, since there was nowhere to escape. I learned that the publisher had sometimes hit her, that he was stingy, that the mistrust and hatred between them went deep. But all this precious intel was buried in her last shocking declaration. This lovely creature, burning with fury from head to toe at the disregard of her lawful ownership, informed him that in that case, she had no choice but to share the bed with me. The rest was none of his business.

I've always been superstitious, that if I became close to a stunning beauty, I would meet with disaster. I was also prudent about involvement in any awkward situations worthy of a screwball comedy. But here I was, embroiled in such a comedy involving such a woman. After hanging up, she looked a lot calmer.

She said, "I can't sleep because I'm jet-lagged, and I'm a lit-tle hungry, too. Do you have anything like ramen around?"

If I hadn't anticipated anything like, "I'm so furious I can't stand it—go shower quickly and come to bed," I also hadn't expected her to merely ask for ramen. After freshening her makeup in the bathroom, she ate the ramen I made. After I set the empty bowl in the sink, I opened a bottle of wine. The wine meant to lift my spirits and keep my hands busy ended up taking us late into the night. Our conversation reached as far as the deepest buried secrets of married couples. I'm hope-less when it comes to seducing women, but I've always ex-celled at conversation.

The woman and I shared the same last name, Bak, and her first name was Yeong-seon. Our common enemy was the publisher. We drank enough to lose count of the empty bot-tles, and—who knew who made the first move?—we ended up collapsing into bed together. It was noon when I woke up. So she was a woman who unconditionally stuck to her word. She was lying next to me, her naked figure so stun-ning that to view it as a mere human body was an insult. Af-ter I briefly gave thanks to the Almighty Creator's omnipo-tence and eternal love, I put my underwear back on and lit a cigarette in the bathroom. I couldn't remember what had happened, but I was certain we had done something irre-versible. When I returned, God's gift was still draped across the bed.

An irresistible force pulled me toward the desk. There, I opened up a new Word document on my laptop for the novel that didn't exist yet. I placed my fingers on the keyboard. That was as far as I'd gotten, but this time my fingers took on a life of their own. It was as if tiny brains were attached to my fingertips. Phrases like "I wrote furiously" are reserved for these kinds of moments. Sentences came to me like falling rain. It was as if I were playing one of those games that teaches you how to type. "Earth-Defending Typing Champion Bak Mansu Intercepts the Many Sentences Attacking the Globe!" What was so important about plot or characters in a manuscript that I wouldn't submit anyway?

The scene I wrote for my erotic, abstract, avant-garde novel was about a protagonist embarking on bizarre sexual adventures while staying in New York's Chinatown. I wrote furiously until I had a short story of over a hundred manuscript pages, but only two hours had passed when I checked the clock. I hadn't experienced such heights of productivity since my debut. I was bewildered. I wondered, How is this possible —is it okay to actually write this?

The censor in me had stopped functioning, so the narrative continued like a car with worn-out brakes. While imagining the publisher's bewilderment as I handed him the manuscript, I glanced at his drowsing wife from the corner of my eye. My fingers flew over the keyboard.

Late that afternoon, the publisher's wife woke up from jet-lagged sleep and asked, "What are you working so hard at?"

Had we become close enough for her to speak so casually to me?

I said, "My novel."

"That's right. You said you're a novelist."

"I used to be pretty famous. Have you heard of *The Toenail of Death*? That was my debut novel."

It was also the book I was most known for.

"*Die, Toenail*? Never heard of it."

She wrapped the bedsheet around her the way famous American actresses did and came over to me.

She said, "Honey, you're a fast typer."

As she spoke, my fingers continued setting down words.

She asked, "You're not really writing what you're imagining right now, are you? You're not just typing out the national anthem or something like that?"

I didn't respond. Instead, I wrote down a few more sentences. Yeong-seon then gave me a peck on the top of my head.

"Amazing. You're brilliant. You look like you've mastered it. The keyboard's about to crack under your fingers."

I stopped typing. Still I heard the sentences in my head whirring past me.

I shouted at her, "Can you be quiet? Why're you so talkative? Leave me alone so I can write."

Looking surprised, she left me alone. After rustling around, she left, slamming the front door behind her. Whatever. My fingers kept flying.

How much time had passed? When she returned with Chinese takeout, I was still at the desk. No, I was in another world, not in New York or Seoul, but standing with the words at the threshold of everywhere, in every space, the cracks of the world, and the mezzanine of the spirit and the body. She appeared impressed by my first experience of writing at near the speed of light.

She said, "You're really still working away?"

I was sitting at the desk in my underwear, the way I'd been since morning. I hadn't had a single bathroom or water break. She set down the Chinese food and embraced me from behind. Her hands, as soft as silk, drifted across my chest and down to my nuts.

"My God. Look, look at how hard you are," she said. "Were you really like this all morning?"

I'd had no idea till then. She gently stroked me across my bulging underwear as if it were the bulb of a tulip. I realized then that my lower belly was tensed up. It was clear that my blood had been concentrated down there throughout my writing session.

"Forget it," I said. "Can't you please just get out of my way? Don't you see I'm writing?"

But she didn't back off. She maneuvered to conquer me, the way that long ago, the legendary Hwangjini did to Seohwadam. Once she buried her hand inside my underwear and began licking my nipples, I couldn't control myself. I leapt up and turned to her. The chair tumbled backwards. She backed away, assuming I was going to be angry again. Instead, I lifted her high up and tossed her onto the bed. She screamed, and I threw myself on top of her. When our frenzied sex grew louder than the mammoth ventilator, the neighbors complained by rapping against the wall. Even then my hands caressed her all over and imprinted countless, indecipherable sentences across her body. Afterward, we lay in bed and ate the cold Chinese takeout with wine. As if she couldn't believe what had happened, she shook her head and began acting coy.

I said, "How about one more time?"

She burst out laughing and fled to the bathroom. As soon as she disappeared, I returned to the desk. This time I noticed that I was hard again as soon as I sat down. I started writing from where I'd stopped. Since it was an unpublishable, erotic, experimental, disjointed novel, I didn't need to reread what I'd written, and consistency of character wasn't important. Whether it made sense or not, all I had to do was keep writing.

As she emerged from the bathroom, she halted. I stared at her. God had made such a beautiful creature. The cunning woman was damp from head to toe, tempting me. Still, I couldn't get up, because my fingers were moving relentlessly over the keys.

"Again?" she said. "What is this? Honey, are you some kind of freak? How can you keep writing like that without a break?"

"It's weird, but I keep wanting to write. I can't stop."

My eyes were caressing her damp body, but my fingers kept flying madly over the keyboard.

"Do you know how many men have told me that they'd have all their wishes fulfilled if they could sleep with me just once?"

"Yeah, I do feel grateful for that. But you might be the reason why I'm able to write like this—see, this has never happened to me before. So you should be proud."

"If so, that's kind of rewarding. Then what should I be doing?"

"Stay just as you are and lie down. That's what I need."

The same situation replayed itself the next day, and the day after that. She left the house to meet friends and go shopping, but it made no difference, since I was completely absorbed in finishing the novel. In the apartment with roaming rats, I did nothing but write until my stomach was sore from the tension. My body and spirit underwent a chemical change. It might have been the epiphany I'd dreamed of, the moment that all artists seek so desperately. The muse had descended.

Only now I was certain that I'd become a true artist. Earlier, I'd merely gone through the motions of being a writer. I'd had a lucky start when my debut book became a wild success, and I was respected as a writer everywhere I went. I'd assumed that this was what being a writer was. I'd written reluctantly only to meet deadlines, and submitted manuscripts as I suppressed my uneasiness. But I'd made a 180-degree reversal. The novel-in-progress and its main character were leading me. It elevated me to a level that I had never attained. When a reporter once asked Stephen King how he could be so prolific, he replied, "I would like to ask a different question. What the hell do other writers do with their time if they don't write every day?" He had already achieved that level. He'd already experienced this rapture. Like him, I had also finally overcome a long slump and entered a new level. I saw now that there were only two types of writers: those who write furiously from a place of ecstasy, such as Stephen King or Balzac, and now me; and those who unfortunately are unable to — meaning writers who regularly beat themselves up and only meet their deadlines because of pressure from their editor. Before New York, I'd been one of the latter.

Reading my printed-out manuscript further surprised me. I hadn't revised it yet, but there were future radiant gems inside it. It had an unforgettable main character and an original, tension-filled plot that branched out in brilliant confusion like the roots of a sweet potato plant. My Lord, I asked myself, is this truly my creation?

I would subsist on the takeout she brought back. We would relax together in bed, and when she nodded off, I'd sit down at the desk and begin typing. It sounds impossible, but I didn't sleep for ten days. I only drowsed a few times on the toilet. Intense sex and crazed writing sessions, that was it. The following scene and others like it repeated themselves: A stark-naked beauty emerges from the bathroom on all fours, edging toward me as I pound away at the desk. I beg, "Please don't get any closer. Can't you see I'm writing?" as I compulsively try to get down a few more sentences. But finally she arrives at my desk and takes my erect penis in her mouth and enjoys herself. When I can't resist any longer, I lift her up and throw her onto the bed. Soon after, I return to the desk.

Who's going to sympathize with the fact that having heated sex with a peerless beauty was actually a heartrending effort to return to the desk?

After ten days passed, I crept into bed with her. She wrinkled her nose and said, "Honey, you smell."

I realized I hadn't showered once during that time.

She added, "You're like an animal."

I said, "Should I shower first?"

"No, I like you this way."

We had passionate sex again. And for the first time in ten days, I fell asleep.

7

"Hey! Hey!" a voice shouted.

Someone was poking at my temple. I'd been deeply asleep and wasn't sure at first whether I was in New York or Seoul. I didn't realize that what I'd dimly heard was a man speaking my native language. I opened my eyes. The intruder turned on the light and the room went bright.

The man said, "Get up, boy."

It was Raccoon. There was no mistaking him, especially under the light. Yeong-seon pressed close to me. She must have been awake.

"What are you doing?" I asked, heart pounding.

He yelled, "That's what I want to ask you. What the hell are you doing? With another man's wife, huh?" He leveled his right hand.

Yeong-seon gasped and held back a scream with her hand. The gun he held resembled the cross in a fanatic's grip. I thought frantically about the many men who had slept with married women and ended up shot to death by jealous husbands. If there's one experience to avoid in a lifetime, it's this: waking up naked to an unpleasant conversation with an uninvited guest.

"Don't do this. It's not his fault," Yeong-seon pleaded. "Mr. Bak finally fell asleep just now. He didn't sleep at all for ten days and just wrote."

"Hmm, and you expect me to believe that?" The publisher's Glock shook before my eyes.

I said, "It's true. It was as if I'd been blessed with words suddenly raining down on me. I really wrote like a madman."

"Don't lie to me! How can you write with a woman like her beside you? You think I don't know what she's like? You must've stayed in bed the whole ten days. It's obvious." He looked at her. "You dirty bitch nympho sex maniac."

"This is a misunderstanding!" I said. "Look, when I'm writing I develop an innately chaste constitution and am incapable of getting a hard-on. All the blood rushes to my head, and I can't get hard—it's common for people who use their head a lot, like writers. That's what it is. The only reason I was lying here is because there's one bed. In fact, it's the first time in ten days I've put my head to the pillow. It's the truth."

He picked up the wastebasket beside the bed. It was brimming with used condoms. He slammed it down and, waving the gun in the air, began shouting at Yeong-seon. Seeing the sperm-filled condoms seemed to fuel his fury. He went through a litany of curses too crass to repeat. Yeong-seon repeatedly cried and begged, but he continued raging. Apparently she had regularly lured men home with her when they lived in New York.

I crept out of bed and returned with the printed copy of the draft.

"Here, this is my manuscript. Please have a look. I'll admit something unseemly did occur between us, but I worked hard on the book. Of course, you'll need to keep in mind that it hasn't been revised . . ."

He looked skeptical. He raised the gun and said, "You two sit there facing the wall. It's a rough neighborhood, so if I kill you both and take off, it'll be seen as the work of a robber. You share the same last name, so the NYPD will think you're married. They won't come up with complicated scenarios like adultery. *CSI* and the like—don't trust the way it looks on TV. A third of the murder cases in the States are unsolved. You know why? Because the killers use guns. Get moving—why aren't you by the wall?"

We sat against the wall as he had commanded, clumsily wrapped in bedsheets. Yeong-seon extended her hand out of the sheet; I held it. I'd once done research for a novel I was working on about murder cases and learned that over 87 percent of murders in America are committed by men. What's more, most of their victims are men—75 percent to be exact.

Men normally kill other men, but why? The reason's obvious. There's always a woman involved. I remember an even more chilling statistic. In Canada, out of the number of wives murdered, as many as 63 percent were those who'd demanded a separation from their husband. The scenario before me was a classic example from a manual of violent crime.

The publisher appeared to be reading my manuscript. I'd never been so nervous having someone read my work. An editor with a gun in his hand: this situation might be what all editors dream of. The editor would break into the house of a lazy writer who was screwing around and not meeting deadlines, and after seizing his draft, immediately hold a trial. If the book was a masterpiece, the editor would let the writer live, and if it was rubbish, he'd be killed. And what about an audacious writer who hadn't bothered to complete a draft? He'd be shot on the spot. *Bang!* There's a saying in the Mafia that goes, "You get a lot more from a kind word and a gun than from a kind word alone."

Outside of the whirring of the ventilator, the only sound was the turning of pages. It was a good sign that he hadn't tossed the manuscript out after reading the opening page. When I first debuted, I'd watched Suji reading my drafts much like this, and agonized while analyzing her every reaction. If she was silent, I'd worry that it wasn't entertaining; if she shifted in her seat, I'd wonder if she was bored and had become anxious. Then at some point, Suji stopped reading my drafts altogether.

Time crawled. I sat in silence and waited for him to finish reading. Each time I wondered if he was drowsing, I heard the page turn. Each time I felt more at ease, as if a tyrant had granted me another day to live.

"Mr. Bak." The Raccoon finally called for me. His voice was more subdued than before. Could this be the power of literature, to purge a man's violent emotional state?

"Yes?"

"What on earth is this story about?"

"Why? Is it boring?"

"No, it's not boring. But I'm asking what it's about."

"It's enough that you enjoyed reading it. Does it matter what it's about?"

"When does the Japanese colonial period circus troupe part come out? So far it's entirely an erotic story."

"Um, it changed, in the direction of *Ulysses*."

He snorted. "Does this happen often in the publishing industry?"

"Of course. Books written as planned are popular fiction and genre. Books that arrive from somewhere unexpected, beyond the writer's intentions—that's literature. That's how it's always been."

"No, I'm talking about a publisher's wife and a writer getting it on." His tone was threatening again.

I said carefully, "That's probably not so common."

"Right?"

"How about a publisher who sleeps with his editor?" I cautiously went on the offensive. "Is that common?"

"How would I know? I'm new to the publishing world."

"You don't know?"

"I said I don't know."

I wasn't the one with the gun, so I backed off.

"Oh," he said, "so you thought that Ms. Lee and I had that kind of relationship. How asinine. Why would someone like me want that kind of relationship with your ex-wife? Oh, but

I heard that Ms. Lee is seeing someone else. Do you know him? A philosophy professor who writes poetry."

Shocked, I shouted, "A philosophy professor who writes poetry? Are you sure?"

"So you know him?

"Ms. Lee brought me a poetry manuscript, saying we'd publish it. Something felt off, so I looked into it and found out about them."

"What—the son of a bitch."

"It sounds like you know each other, but right now doesn't seem the time to be angry . . ."

I recalled how my philosophy friend kept asking me about my ex and her boss. What was this? He'd said, "Is Suji really that amazing a woman?" The asshole had been playing with me. If I say something, he'll calmly tell me about how Suji and he were merely dealing with the weighty "concept of sex." I needed a gun too. I wanted to ask Philosophy: Can your weighty concept actually defeat the agility and speed of a bullet?

The publisher tossed my draft onto the desk.

"Now let's forget about it. It's not as if you'll make it back alive. Here are my thoughts on your novel. It's garbage. This novel you've written to make a fool of me—what the hell's your real motive for writing it?"

"Garbage? I don't understand. Of course, I agree that my initial motive for writing it was dishonest—I mean, my motive was unclear. But once I started, something mysterious happened. To some extent all writers experience how a novel ends up betraying its writer. This time, my novel transcended me, went beyond my miserable problems and my limited imagination and took me to an extraordinary place.

This manuscript wasn't written by me, Bak Mansu, but it borrowed my hands—the way Jesus borrowed Mary's body and came into the world—and is being born into the world right now. You might object to my Christian language; maybe a Son Buddhist monk would say you've become enlightened, or something like that."

"You're trying to scam me now, since I'm just a Wall Street guy who fooled around with money."

"That isn't it."

"Do you know what my job was at Goldman Sachs?"

"Not really." All that had stuck was the acronym OPM.

"It was calculating the exact market value of bonds. Know what bonds are? Put simply, it's debt. When it came to bonds, I made no mistakes. When I bought out this damn publishing firm, it turned out the thing was entirely built on debt. Bad debt created by these writers who gobble up their advances and don't turn in their manuscripts. And you're the worst of the worst."

"That's a little extreme . . ."

"You even screwed my wife. You think this debt's easy to pay off now? Outside of death . . ." He was overexcited and began stuttering. "Yeah, the debt's only payable with de-death."

"Since you're reading with that kind of bias . . ."

"You think I got a large salary at Goldman Sachs by being biased while calculating bond values? I'm a cool-headed person."

"I'm telling you, this novel is different!"

"Remember, I've read all your novels. Honestly, I did rather like them. But this one lacks even the few merits of the others. It's complete shit."

Yeong-seon said, "That's not true."

He said, "What's this? You read it, too? But you don't know anything about fiction."

I was as surprised as he was. I had no idea that she'd been reading it.

She said, "You're the one who doesn't understand fiction. From a man who knows nothing but money . . . I used to read quite a lot of novels, though that changed once I married your kind."

I said, "Anyway, what did you think?"

A writer always wants to hear his readers' opinions, whether the readers are naked or fully dressed.

These words emerged from her lovely lips: "You're right. I don't know literature, but this novel knocked me out. Frankly, I didn't really grasp the main character's ideas, and I had no idea what direction the plot was going, but once I picked it up, I couldn't put it down. It's like taking a long drag of good pot."

I asked, "What's pot?"

The publisher answered instead, saying, "You don't know pot and you call yourself a writer? It's cannabis. Marijuana."

"At the least, he was working incredibly hard. And typing so fast. He didn't even sleep, he was up all night—"

I was petrified that she would bring up the mysterious state of that one body part, but thankfully she had enough sense not to.

"It was like he was possessed. Writing in that state, whatever comes out will truly be something else. Be honest, you were completely hooked, too."

Raccoon frowned. "You two must have different literary

taste from mine. Not all lunacy is artistic fire. Praying loudly and speaking in tongues don't make a saint. Trashy fiction can read well, too. Also, what makes a writer a master of his craft? Does typing speed matter? I'll publish the book as Bak Man-su's final novel. If I publicize it as your posthumous work, I'll be able to recover the advance, and if I'm lucky, it may even be a bestseller. Or would it sell better if the media talked it up as your novel-in-progress when you were murdered in New York? It looks like you've written well over a hundred manuscript pages, which is enough for a book, and since a shoddy second half doesn't exist, readers can make up their own ending. They might feel disappointed. They might say, 'It could have been a masterpiece.' No matter how I look at it, dying about now is the best solution. Mr. Bak, your death will also help the fate of your books."

"But aren't you curious about what happens next? Didn't Yeong-seon also say that it was a riveting read? First give me a chance to finish writing the book."

"A book requires a plot to keep a reader curious," he declared. It was amusing enough, but once I put it down, I lost interest. I'm more curious about what's happening in this room right now. You see, I've dreamed of killing Yeong-seon for years—you've no idea for how long." He looked at his wife. "I've killed you countless times in my mind. I've even attempted to go through with it. But each time, my plan was flawed. So each time I revised it, then revised it again, but only now does it look perfect. Planning a murder is a little like contemplating immigration. Once you start thinking about it, you can't stop."

Yeong-seon snapped, "You think I've never wanted to kill

you, too? You always think you're right. You think your plans look perfect this time? You'd be digging your own grave. If I die, you'll be the prime suspect. Immigration's also got a record of your entry."

"I've already established the perfect alibi, don't worry."

Before they became even more riled up, I interrupted. "A perfect alibi? That itself is an illusion. There's always a flaw. About writers, those who start with perfectly outlined novels rarely ever write anything worthwhile. They fail because once you start writing, the characters take on a life of their own and the work goes in an entirely different direction. The way I see it, you've got an obsessive personality. Like a kid who believes that once he's made a plan, he has to stick to it. Now, let's put the gun down. You can't reverse murder. You don't want to end up doing something so reckless. Life isn't a game."

"Shut up! All you do is talk. If you know so much, why are your novels such a mess?" He raised the pistol again. "Now let me make you an offer you can't refuse."

He reached into his pocket and tossed two packets of medicine at us.

"You don't seem too hot on the gun, so I'll give you a choice. Either take the meds or take the bullet."

I said, "What is it?"

"The fun part here is that you don't know. It could be cyanide, it could be sleeping pills. If you don't take the pills, I'll pull the trigger without hesitation. No need to worry—no one'll call the cops in this neighborhood."

"Wait a minute," said Yeong-seon. "If we take this, we could die, right?"

"Right."

"Do you really have to kill me? You pathetic man."

"I do. I can't put up with you anymore. Actually, I can't endure my desire to kill you anymore."

"I'll give you a divorce. I mean it this time."

"A divorce costs too much. Besides, all my planning would be wasted then, wouldn't it?"

"Bastard," she said.

"Curse me all you want—especially since you don't have much time left for that."

I sneaked a look at her lovely profile as she bit her lip. Would Raccoon really put an end to such a gorgeous creature? She adopted an innocent, modest pose with her legs folded together, looking outright tragic as she clutched the packet of pills. A guy who'd made it on Wall Street was truly different. His bargaining skills defeated us. Do you want to choose A or B—a 100 percent certain death with the gun, or the pills that at least give you a chance? But if the pills were poisonous, they would clearly be a killer's preferred method. It would be an unquestioned suicide. The plot was no good for a novel, but it was pretty useful in real life.

"I have one last request," I said. "I ask that you give my unfinished novel full attention during the editing and copy-editing. For your reference, Suji knows best how to edit my work."

He tossed a pen and a piece of paper at me. "I told you, taking the meds doesn't mean that you'll die for sure. Look, let's make a pact first. If you take the meds and survive, let's agree that today never happened. We'll put it down as a reckless joke. I'll leave you two alone, and you won't do anything like report this to the police. Deal? Now, let's put it down on paper."

"I'll write it, I'll write it." I quickly grabbed the pen.

"I'll dictate."

I tightened my grip on the pen.

"I forgive everything," he recited. "I forgive even the unforgivable, so please also forgive me for what I've done."

I complained, "But it sounds too much like a suicide note."

"I guess it's possible to see it that way."

He smirked and aimed the gun at my forehead. "Now write!"

I had no choice but to write down what he told me. Now that he had a suicide note, his plan was flawless. Only then did I truly see him. He wasn't a man raging after his wife had cheated on him. Every piece of the plot fitted seamlessly. Now that I think of it, the English word "plot" translates into "conspiracy" or "structure" in Korean. Criminals and writers have something in common that way. They covertly formulate a plan and execute it. They also share the fact that if the plan is obvious, they both get caught. Also, both can be betrayed by their own wits. You could say that the novel I'd been writing lacked structure and had no plot. In contrast, the publisher's plot felt like a well-structured—and therefore vulgar—mystery novel. And yet it's the publisher who comes out ahead. Could this mean that a well-constructed plot will ultimately win over a plotless narrative? Am I leaping to conclusions? I gazed at Yeong-seon, who was quietly preparing for her death. The last puzzle piece in this crime-of-passion story is the stunning femme fatale. But this woman seems too resigned for someone facing imminent death.

"Wait a minute!" I lifted my hand.

The publisher said, "What is it this time?"

"Can I switch pills with your wife?"

"Why?"

"If they're the same pills, it won't matter whether we switch. Can I do that? And if I can't, why not?"

He frowned. "You sure you won't regret it?"

Yeong-seon gripped her packet and didn't let go.

"Hand that over," I said, and snatched hers away and swapped.

He said, "You think the ending will be any different now?"

"Possibly . . ."

"Hmm. You know what your problem is? You don't take life seriously enough. You think you're writing this novel? Here you're not a writer but a character! A dependent variable, you understand?"

When I ripped open the packet, a single white pill rolled out.

"Now, swallow the pill. This time I'm really going to shoot. You see, I've got to use the bathroom. Here, I'll count to three. Come on! One, two . . ."

He aimed the gun at me. I shut my eyes tight and shoved the pill in my mouth. As it reached my tongue, the bitter pill began to melt. Look here, Raccoon, you're saying I'm only a character? Nonsense! I'm the writer of the complex, erotic, fragmented novel that is my life. I've got no real story line. I'm also the main character in a story that no one wants to publish. You call me a dependent variable? Absolutely not. I'm the writer and the first-person narrator, and I'm the one who controls the ending. For this story to end, it's neither you nor your wife but me who has to die. Only then can the words "The End" be written.

But why . . . isn't it ending?

I slowly open my eyes. The room feels as if it has expanded a little. No, it's expanded a lot. The ceiling soars and the hall looks so far away. The apartment's furniture has somehow disappeared. The chair, the bed, even the windows are gone. It's as if I'm in jail. Those stripes, are they barred windows or the wallpaper pattern? I turn toward the publisher. He looks strange, as if he is slowly becoming something else. A red cockscomb is growing out of the top of his head, and his lips begin jutting out until they become a beak. Next to me, I hear flapping sounds. Yeong-seon is also transforming. Her thin arms become wings; her lovely feet split into three parts. Two enormous chickens stare fiercely down at me. I tremble with fright. I become smaller and the room, bigger. The two chickens raise their heads and make strange clucking sounds. I'm afraid. I'm so afraid.

Finally a sentence breaks out of the hazy fog of my consciousness and slowly begins to take shape. I read the sentence aloud to myself:

I am not a cob of corn.

I am not a cob of corn.

I am not a cob . . .

And yet I keep thinking that this isn't enough.